成語諺語
精選300則

上野潤子　著

大新書局　印行

序 言

　　成語諺語是流傳於市井街衢的一種言簡意賅的修辭表現，它是根據先民們的生活經驗累積而成的智慧結晶，它是基於民眾的細密觀察而雕琢成的創作詞句，它是民族的文化思想凝縮而成的哲學邏輯。當中有些詞句雖然乍聽之下通俗淺顯，但一語雙關、耐人尋味，寥寥數字即能點到為止。由於成語諺語廣泛地應用於日常生活中，自然地發展出許多反映出社會百態，價值觀和民族思想的獨特內涵。有不落俗套的隱喻，也有不甚含蓄的直喻；有鼓舞的啟示，也有刺耳的批評；有幽默的措辭表現，也有嚴肅的教誨訓誡。

　　成語主要以文言形式，諺語多半以口語形式表達。成語諺語所以能流傳久遠，是因為它易懂易記、寓意深遠，對世道人心有潛移默化的功用。同時，成語諺語乃文學作品和語言的精華之一，有其不可或缺的一席地位。不論男女老幼，不論權貴平民，於文章和談話中屢見成語諺語之引用，使措辭更具深度，使表達更加生動。

　　然而，成語諺語時常是外語學習中的絆腳石。因為文化背景不同，成語諺語的含義和用法不易理解。若能在母語中找到對應的近義成語或諺語，問題就可迎刃而解。

　　日本民眾一向喜好成語諺語，自古由史籍和繪畫中可看出端倪。2011 年日本的文部科學省新編的「小學校學習指導要領」中強調傳統文化教育的重要性，將成語諺語・慣用語列入學習重點之一，規定小學三年級的國語課程編入成語諺語的教學時數。各高中大學和社會人士組織有成語諺語研究社團和學會等，甚至還有全國性檢定考試(2011 年開始)，以喚醒年輕人對成語諺語的興趣。

　　本書精選出 300 句日本人皆可隨口而出、歷久彌新的成語諺語。其中有一部分的修辭源自漢語或英語文化圈，但已融入日本文化，演變成日本人生活中常用的詞彙和語句，亦有一小部分的修辭經過長年累月的翻譯後，喻義已與漢文或英文的原意略有不同或迥然不同。本書每一詞句皆附日語、漢語和英語解釋與用法說明，有助於自學的讀者正確地理解成語諺語的含義，從而切實地應用於文章或談話中。

　　著者出生於臺灣，高中畢業後旅居日本屆 40 餘年，透過長年和日本人生活相處的體會，無形中對日語文化圈的成語諺語產生好奇心。2008 年加入「日本ことわざ文化學會」，參與成語諺語的研究考證和出版編輯工作。

　　本書不但對於談論、閱讀或寫作能力有所助益，也希望藉由學習成語諺語的機會，順便讓我們更理解日本人的文化思想、風俗習慣和禮俗儀節，進一步能對其民族性有更多的體認，以促進彼此之間的交流。

著者　於東京寒舍

編撰說明

一．適用對象：初級以上的日語學習者。

二．編撰目的：提昇日語的說、寫、讀的能力，有助於參加大學日語學科入
學甄試、日語能力測驗或日系企業就職應試等。

三．編撰內容：

1．收錄有常用成語諺語 300 則，全為日本國中學生耳熟能詳的成語或諺語。

2．詞句依首字的 50 音排序，若首字的音同，依次字的 50 音排序，其餘依
此類推。

3．每則成語或諺語詞句的編撰方針分項如下：

(1)每則成語或諺語，明記漢字的平假名注音，並標明難易度的級數。級
數乃根據日本諺語檢定協會和普及版國文教科書所定的基準。然而，
依專家觀點不同級數的分級標準頗有差距。同時，因時代變遷，有部
分詞句難免產生措辭上的變異，例如採用不同的漢字或不同的表記，
本書乃依據正宗辭典中最通用的表記。每則詞句列舉近似的成語或諺
語，以 近義詞 示之。若無則示以 --。江戶至明治時代紙牌遊戲中常見
的成語或諺語以 * 記號註明。

(2)日解與用法──以 日解與用法 示之。每則詞句的意義和用法加以日語解說
粗筆畫為按原文字面上的含義直譯，非粗筆畫則為意譯或引申義。解
說中竭力使用自然的句型、不同的單字，並盡量採用慣用語法來說明，
以增加學習語彙的機會。

(3)漢解與用法──以 漢 示之。每則詞句的意義和用法加以漢語解說，粗筆
畫為直譯，非粗筆畫則為引申義。考慮到文化角度不同，解說內容不
一定完全依照日解的說法。

(4)英解與用法──以 英 示之。每則詞句的意義和用法加以英語解說，粗筆
畫為直譯，非粗筆畫則為引申義。考慮到文化角度不同，解說內容不
一定完全依照日解的說法。

(5)漢語近義成語或諺語──以[近]示之。每則詞句列舉近似的漢語成語或諺語，若無則示以 --。

(6)英語近義成語或諺語──以[近]示之。每則詞句列舉近似的英語成語或諺語，若無則示以 --。

(7)漢語字體以繁體字為準，英語拼字以美式英語為準。

4. 依50音排序附日語索引便於讀者快速查找詞句，索引不但含300則成語諺語的關鍵句，亦含蓋文中列舉的近義成語或諺語，也含解說中引用的成語或諺語。漢語索引依筆劃，英語索引則依照字母次序排列。

本書編撰嚴謹並經專家校閱過，但難免百密一疏，盼讀者不吝賜教，俾再版時據以更正。另外，為了尊重原文的措辭，本書中也許含有少數不登大雅、不合時宜或展現偏見的用語，請讀者體諒包涵。

點選書眉，會唸出該書眉。

點選題號、日文成語或諺語，會唸出該則成語或諺語。

點選日文句子，會唸出該句子。

あ行

19 絵に描いた餅* 6級
（え　か　　　もち）

日解與用法 絵に描かれた餅は、美味しそうに見え
（え　か　　　もち　　　　おい　　　み）
晴らしい計画を立てても、実現しな
（　　　けいかく　た　　　　　じつげん）
ない構想、実現する見込みのない目
（　　こうそう　じつげん　　　みこ　　　　　もく）

近義詞 机上の空論 5級 畳の上の水練 4級
（きじょう　くうろん）　（たたみ　うえ　　すいれん）

漢 畫裏繪的餅即使描繪得維妙維肖也不
能充饑，派不上用場。比喻虛名或空
想是沒有實際用處的。也比喻渺茫的
希望。

英 A ri
us

空中樓閣；畫餅不能充饑，望梅□

點選每則近義詞，會唸出該則近義詞。

點選 近義詞 ，會唸出條列的所有近義詞。

點選 日解與用法 ，會唸出該則的日文解釋和用法。

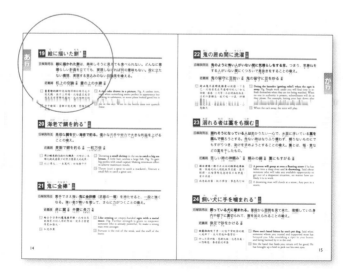

5

目　次

第一章

日本的國中升學考試出題率最高的成語諺語
100則（50音排序）

100 Need-to-know Idioms and Proverbs
for Junior High Graduates

1 悪事千里を走る 6級

日解與用法 悪いことをしたという評判は遠くまでも広がる。悪いことはあっという間に世間に知れ渡ることから、悪いことをしてはいけない、という教訓。中国の成語に由来。

近義詞 悪い噂は翼を持つ 4級

漢 壞事傳播千里遠。比喻愈不名譽的事，別人知道得愈快。勸人不要做壞事，因為壞的口碑一傳十，十傳百，一下子傳遍街坊鄰里，難以遏止。

近 (好事不出門) 惡事行千里

英 Bad deeds run a thousand ri (borrowed from a Chinese proverb, a "ri" is a distance unit equal to 2.44 miles). Bad news spreads in no time at all. Suggests that someone avoids doing wrong as people have a tendency to enjoy spreading bad news amongst the people they know.

近 Bad news travels fast.; Ill news comes apace.

2 頭隠して尻隠さず* 6級

日解與用法 キジが草むらに頭を突っ込んで全身を隠したつもりでいるが、尻尾は丸見えになっている。欠点や悪いことの一部だけ隠して、自分では全部を隠したつもりでいる様子をあざ笑っていう言葉。

近義詞 雉の草隠れ 4級　柿を盗んで核を隠さず 3級

漢 只顧藏頭卻沒有遮掩臀部。譏笑一個愚昧的人想掩蓋缺點或壞事的真相，結果自暴其短，欲蓋彌彰。(註：與漢語「藏頭露尾」的意思略有不同)

近 掩耳盜鈴；自欺欺人

英 To ridicule someone's attempt to hide one's head but leave one's rear end exposed, thinking they can cover up defect or knavery.

近 You dance in a net and think nobody sees you.

3 後の祭り 6級

日解與用法 祭りの後の祭り屋台や神輿は役に立たない。良い機会を逃してどうにもしようのないこと。手遅れになって、取り返しがつかなくなることをいう。

近義詞 六日の菖蒲十日の菊 4級　証文の出し遅れ 4級

漢 慶典活動後的花車派不上用場。比喻錯失良機，或比喻事後的張羅、無濟於事。

近 雨後送傘；賊去關門；過了黃梅買簑衣；蘇州過後無艇搭

英 To bring out the float after the festival has finished. Said when you missed out on a chance that you will really regret later. With the wisdom of hindsight, people realize they acted too late.

近 (A) day after the fair.; After meat, mustard.; After death, the doctor.; (a) day late and a dollar short

4 後は野となれ山となれ 6級

日解與用法 自分が立ち去った後は、その場所が**野になろうとも、山になろうとも**気にしない。今ある問題が片付いてしまえば、後はどうなっても構わない。当面のことさえ良ければ、これから先のことは、自分の知ったことではないということの喩え。

近義詞 末は野となれ山となれ 3級

漢 管它以後變成荒野還是山林，眼前的事情解決即可，身後之事如何演變管不了那麼多了，隨它去吧！

近 只圖今日有飯吃，不圖下世沒柴燒；管他三七二十一

英 **Let it be a wild moor or a mountain**; Fig. I don't care what follows after I'm gone, even if the whole world is destroyed. Let whatever events come to pass. When you take care of the present the future takes care of itself.

近 After us the deluge.; Come what may. (Macbeth)

5 虻蜂取らず 6級

日解與用法 **虻と蜂の両方を**捕まえようとして、二つとも**取り逃してしまう**ように、欲張って二つのものを同時に手に入れようとすると、結局はどちらも得られないことをいう。

近義詞 二兎を追う者は一兎をも得ず* 6級　花も折らず実も取らず 4級

漢 想捉馬蠅又想捉蜜蜂，結果什麼都得不到。貪多必失，告誡人不要太貪婪，免得兩頭落空。

近 雞飛蛋打；務廣而荒

英 **To catch neither the horsefly nor the wasp**; Used as a warning that you will achieve neither of the two aims if you are too greedy. Don't try to do two things at once.

近 Grasp all, lose all.; fall between two stools; If you run after two hares, you will catch neither.

6 雨降って地固まる* 6級

日解與用法 雨が降った後は、地面が乾くと固く締まり、前よりよい状態になる。争いの後は、かえって以前より良い関係になることの喩え。もめごとが起こると、それを解決するために話し合い、お互いが理解し合うようになる。

近義詞 喧嘩の後の兄弟名乗り 3級　諍い果てての契り 3級

漢 雨後地湿，愈吵愈親。比喻爭吵後當事者雙方的感情反而比以前融洽。

近 不打不成交；不打不相識

英 **Ground cemented after the rain.** Said that a relationship can become even stronger after a conflict or tough times.

近 After a storm comes a calm.; The quarrel of lovers is the renewal of love.

7 案ずるより産むが易し 6級

日解與用法 出産は事前に思い悩むほど、難しくないということから、物事は実際に行ってみると、意外に簡単なことと実感する。取り越し苦労をしても仕方ない、という励ましの言葉。

近義詞 案じるより団子汁 3級

漢 生小孩比牽掛的容易，比喻凡事通常比憂慮的還要簡單，任何問題都自然會找到解決方法，先做再說，不須過早擔心。

近 車到山前必有路，船到橋頭自然直

英 **Giving birth is sometimes easier than worrying about a safe delivery.** Fig. Doing something often turns out to be easier than it seemed beforehand, therefore, don't worry about something that has not happened yet. You never know till you try.

近 All things are difficult before they are easy.; Care is no cure.; Let's cross that bridge when we come to it.

8 石の上にも三年* 6級

日解與用法 冷たい石の上にも三年座り続ければ石が暖かくなる意。辛抱強く苦しみに耐えれば、いつかきっと成功するという。継続は力なり。弛まず挫けず、続けていくことの大切さを述べている。

近義詞 茨の中にも三年 3級　商い三年 3級

漢 石頭坐上三年才會暖和。鍥而不捨持之以恆，才能有所成就。

近 只要功夫深，鐵杵磨成針；愚公移山；有志者事竟成；皇天不負苦心人

英 **Even the cold rock will get warm if is sat on for three years.** Encourages people to stick with one's goal while perseverance wins in the end; A brilliant achievement requires tenacity and endurance. Persistence pays off.

近 Perseverance prevails.; Energy and persistence conquer all things.; Patience and application will carry us through.

9 石橋を叩いて渡る 6級

日解與用法 丈夫な石の橋なのに、叩いて安全であることを確かめて渡る。用心の上にも用心して物事を行う様子を言う。慎重すぎる人、臆病な人や決断の鈍い人に対して皮肉をこめて使う場合もある。

近義詞 浅い川も深く渡れ 4級　瀬を踏んで淵を知る 3級

漢 敲著石橋過河。形容辦事萬分謹慎，連堅固的石橋也一步一步小心謹慎地渡過。

近 摸著石頭過河；投石問路；小心翼翼；三思而後行；步步為營

英 **Tapping a stone bridge** to test its sturdiness **while crossing it**; To watch one's step with extreme caution; To consider all aspects of a situation before one takes action; To behave too cautiously, not taking any chances.

近 Look before you leap.; test the water(s)

10 急がば回れ* 6級

日解與用法 急ぐ時には、危険な近道より、時間がかかっても**無難な道を通る**方が結局早く目的地に着く。慌てず、安全で着実な方法を取れ、という戒め。

近義詞 急いては事を仕損じる* 6級　近道は遠道 5級

漢 提醒人急事緩辦。寧願花時間繞道走安全的路，比冒險走捷徑更早抵目的地。

近 以迂為直；寧走十步遠，不走一步險

英 **If you're in a rush, make a detour.** Do things the proper way instead of hurriedly and heedlessly.

近 Make haste slowly.; More haste, less speed.; Slow and steady wins the race.; The longest way round is the shortest way home.

11 一寸の虫にも五分の魂 6級

日解與用法 体長僅か**一寸の虫**でさえ、その半分にあたる**五分の魂がある**。どんな弱い者でもそれなりの意地があるのだから、侮ってはならないという。「一寸」は約 3.03 センチ。

近義詞 蛞蝓にも角 3級　痩せ腕にも骨 3級

漢 一寸的小蟲也有五分的氣魄。不可逼人太甚，即使弱者也會反抗，不容欺侮。

近 (三軍可奪帥也) 匹夫不可奪志也

英 **Even one *sun*-long (*sun*≒1.2 inches) insect has half a *sun* of spirit.** It means that even a meek person will resist or retaliate if pushed too far. Don't humiliate anyone no matter how seemingly weak.

近 Even a worm will turn. Tread on a worm and it will turn.; The lowest trees have tops, the ant her gall, the fly her spleen.

12 犬も歩けば棒に当たる* 6級

日解與用法 **犬がうろつき回ると、棒で叩かれる**。じっとしていれば安全だが、用もなくぶらぶらしていると災難に見舞われるという。本来は否定的意味であった。最近では動き回れば意外な幸運に出くわす、という肯定的意味で用いることが多く見られるようになった。文脈によって意味が変わる。

近義詞 歩く足には棒当たる 4級　歩く足には泥がつく 3級　歩く足には塵がつく 3級

漢 **狗到處亂跑會挨棒打。**①原本帶有負面的意思，比喻安份者沒事，四處遊蕩反而天外飛來橫禍。②現在則常用於正面評價，比喻機動性的人四處奔走，會碰到意料之外的好運。視文章上下文的內容，可以有不同的解釋。

近 ①動不如靜；動輒得咎　②靜不如動；進取逢通達

英 Depending on the context, it can be interpreted either way:
① **If a dog roams, it will eventually bump into a stick.** Fig. If you stroll across the street drifting without purpose, troubles may befall you.
② **If a dog roams, it will find a stick.** Fig. Any assertive action will bring you luck somehow.

近 ① Never go looking for trouble. ② The dog that trots about finds a bone.; Fortune knocks once at every man's door.

13 井の中の蛙大海を知らず* 6級
（い なか かわずたいかい し）

日解與用法 小さな**井戸の中にいる蛙は大きな海がある**ことを**知らない**。見聞が少（ち い ど なか おお うみ し けんぶん すく）なく、世間知らずであることの喩え。中国の成語に由来。（せけんし たと ちゅうごく せいご ゆらい）

近義詞 井蛙は以て海を語るべからず 3級　夏虫、氷を疑う 1級（せいあ もっ うみ かた か ちゅう こおり うたが）

漢 小井裏的青蛙不知大海有多濶。比喻一個人孤陋寡聞，思路狹窄，見識編淺。

近 井底之蛙，不識大海；坐井觀天；目光如豆

英 A frog in a well knows nothing of the great ocean (borrowed from a Chinese proverb). If a person has been living in a very small community for their whole life, he or she can't see things from a wider perspective. Often used to denote that a person who has a narrow world view based on his/her limited experience.

近 He that stays in the valley shall never get over the hill.; Homekeeping youths have ever homely wits.

14 言わぬが花 6級
（い はな）

日解與用法 あからさまに言うと差し障りがある時は、口に出して**言わない方が**奥ゆかしい(品・趣がある)。時と場合によって、黙っている方がかえって値打ちがあるものだという意。（ひん おもむき とき ばあい だま ほう ねう）

近義詞 沈黙は金、雄弁は銀 6級　言わぬは言うに勝る 3級（ちんもく きん ゆうべん ぎん い い まさ）

漢 含而不露，不說反而像花一樣高雅。引申為辭達則止，不貴多言。因為言多必失，有些事情不宜一五一十地全盤托出，說破有時不但傷感情，到頭來又要後悔。

近 不說為妙 / 妙在不言中；江湖一點訣，說破不值錢

英 That left unsaid is as elegant as the flower (Better leave it unsaid); Fig. Sometimes it's better to keep one's mouth shut than say something and regret it later.

近 Silence is golden.; Silence is more eloquent than words.; Better to remain silent and be thought a fool than to speak out and remove all doubt. (Abraham Lincoln); The heart of a fool is in his mouth, but the mouth of a wise man is in his heart. (Benjamin Franklin)

15 魚心あれば水心 6級
（うおごころ みずごころ）

日解與用法 **魚が水に親しむ心を持てば、水もその魚に好意を持つ**こと。相手が好（さかな みず した こころ も みず さかな こうい も あいて こう）意を見せれば、自分も好意を持って対応しようとすることの喩え。（み じぶん こうい も たと）

近義詞 落花流水の情 4級　太鼓もばちの当たりよう 3級（らっかりゅうすい じょう たいこ あ）

漢 魚若有心水也有意。比喻對方若以誠懇相待，自己也以友好的態度回報。

近 魚幫水水幫魚；禮尚往來；人情一把鋸，你不來，我不去

英 If a fish is friendly toward water, water will reciprocate its kindness. If you genuinely like somebody, they will like you back. If you do a favor for somebody, you will get a return favor.

近 You scratch my back and I'll scratch yours.; You roll my log and I'll roll yours.; Kindness lies not aye in one side of the house.

16 嘘も方便 6級

日解與用法 嘘は悪いことであるが、物事を円滑に運ぶためには、**嘘が便利**な時もあり、時に嘘をつかねばならないこともある。本来は仏教の言葉で、衆生を仏の道に導くためには、嘘も止むを得ない、という。

近義詞 嘘も追従も世渡り 3級

漢 謊話有時是為了方便（應變）。在某種情況下不得已的撒謊乃為權宜之計，無傷大雅。據說連佛陀為了使眾生悟道，出於無奈也會撒謊。

近 說謊為權宜之計

英 **Lying is sometimes useful.** It is said that the Buddha claimed that fibbing or telling a white lie is a necessary evil because it could be a tactful and harmless way for preaching. Like a common method called "pious fraud" employed by some early Christian writers. Their intention was to convert anyone by any means available.

近 The end justifies the means.

17 独活の大木 6級

日解與用法 **独活の茎**は生長すると2メートル以上にも達し、**大きくなる**。柔らかいために建材にはならないことから、身体ばかり大きくて何の役にも立たない人をからかっていう言葉。

近義詞 大男総身に知恵が回りかね 4級

漢 **土當歸莖**雖然**大**，但材質軟不能成材。比喻大而無當，人個子高大，中看不中用，一無可取之處。

近 草包虛大漢，能吃不能幹；虛有其表

英 **A big *udo* tree** (*Aralia cordata* - herbaceous plant) **looks large** but is almost good for nothing. A euphemistic way said about a big, clumsy, gawky, slow witted and useless person (such as a big oaf).

近 Mickle head, little wit.

18 馬の耳に念仏* 6級

日解與用法 **馬に念仏**の有難さが分からないように、価値が理解できない者や聞き入れようとしない者に忠告や意見を言い聞かせても、聞く耳を持たず、何の効き目もない。そのようなことをしても無駄だ、ということの喩え。

近義詞 馬の耳に風* 5級　馬耳東風 5級　牛に経文 4級　犬に論語 4級

漢 **對著馬耳唸經**。比喻把別人的話當作耳邊風。對不明理的人、沒興趣的人，講高深的道理，白費力。或比喻對所聽到的事，不加關心，充耳不聞。

近 馬耳東風；對牛彈琴；左耳進，右耳出

英 **Chanting to a horse's ear**; An unavailing attempt to persuade a person who does not wish to listen or does not appreciate it.

近 preach to deaf ears; (be like) talking to a brick wall; go in one ear and out the other; There's none so deaf as those who will not hear.

19 絵に描いた餅* [6級]

日解與用法 絵に描かれた餅は、美味しそうに見えても食べられない。どんなに素晴らしい計画を立てても、実現しなければ何の意味もない。役に立たない構想、実現する見込みのない目論見を喩える。

近義詞 机上の空論 [5級] 畳の上の水練 [4級]

漢 畫裏繪的餅即使描繪得維妙維肖也不能充饑，派不上用場。比喻虛名或空想是沒有實際用處的。也比喻渺茫的希望。

近 空中樓閣；畫餅不能充饑，望梅不能止渴

英 **A rice cake drawn in a picture.** Fig. A useless item, used when something seems perfect in appearance but lacking in substance, or some plans looked good but is unlikely to be achieved.

近 pie in the sky; Wine in the bottle does not quench thirst.

20 海老で鯛を釣る* [6級]

日解與用法 高価な鯛を安い海老で釣る。僅かな元手や労力で大きな利益を上げることの喩え。

近義詞 麦飯で鯉を釣る [4級] 一粒万倍 [4級]

漢 用小蝦米釣值錢的大鯛魚。比喻出小本賺大錢或盡最少的努力獲最大的成果。

近 以小博大；一本萬利；四兩撥千斤

英 Throwing **a small shrimp** in the sea **to catch a big sea bream.** A little bait catches a large fish. Fig. To gain big profits with small capital; Making minimum effort to achieve maximum results.

近 Throw (out) a sprat to catch a mackerel.; Venture a small fish to catch a great one.

21 鬼に金棒* [6級]

日解與用法 素手でさえ強い鬼に金砕棒（武器の一種）を持たせると、一段と強くなる。強い者が勢いを増して、さらに力がつくことの喩え。

近義詞 虎に翼 [5級] 弁慶に長刀 [4級]

漢 給赤手空拳的魔鬼狼牙棒。比喻本來就強有力的人得到幫助，使其力量變得更加強大。

近 如虎添翼

英 **Like arming** an empty-handed **ogre with a metal mace.** Fig. Further strength is given to empower someone who is already powerful; To make a strong man even stronger.

近 Fortune is the rod of the weak, and the staff of the brave.

22 鬼の居ぬ間に洗濯 6級

日解與用法 鬼のように怖い人がいない間に心の洗濯（気晴らし）をする意。つまり、気兼ねをする人がいない間にくつろいで息抜きをすることの喩え。

近義詞 鬼の留守に豆拾い 4級　鬼の留守に豆を炒る 4級

漢 趁凶鬼不在時洗滌身心放鬆一下自己。比喻老是在耳邊嘮叨的人（如父母親，婆婆，上司等）不在時無拘無束，沒有什麼顧忌，就可喘一口氣，紓解壓力。

近 貓兒不在，老鼠做怪；閻王不在，小鬼翻天

英 **Doing the laundry (getting relief) when the ogre is away.** Fig. People work under you will find time to refresh themselves when they are not being watched. When no one in authority is present, subordinates will do as they please. For example, letting your hair down after you've been working hard with your boss all day, or when your mother-in-law or parents are away from home.

近 When the cat's away, the mice will play.

23 溺れる者は藁をも掴む 6級

日解與用法 溺れそうになっている人は助かりたい一心で、水面に浮いている藁を掴んで頼ろうとする。危ない時はなりふり構わず、頼りないものにでもすがりつき、助けを求めようとすることの喩え。藁とは、稲・麦などの茎を干したもの。

近義詞 苦しい時の神頼み* 6級　頼みの綱 6級　藁にもすがる 5級

漢 溺水者連一根浮在水面的稻草也要抓住。快淹死的人胡亂抓草求援，急不暇擇。比喻事勢危急時來不及考慮，盲目求援。

近 病急亂投醫；飢不擇食；事急馬行田

英 **A person will grasp at even a floating straw if he has fallen into a deep river and is drowning.** Said about someone who will take any available opportunity to get out of a desperate situation, no matter how unlikely it is to work.

近 A drowning man will clutch at a straw.; Any port in a storm.

24 飼い犬に手を噛まれる* 6級

日解與用法 飼っている犬に噛まれる。普段から面倒を見て来た、信頼していた身内や部下に裏切られて、害を加えられることの喩え。

近義詞 後足で砂をかける 4級

漢 被寵物狗咬了手。比喻平常縱容的親人或部下，反而背叛和傷害你。

近 好心不得好報；恩將仇報；忘恩負義；以怨報德；養老鼠咬布袋

英 **Have one's hand bitten by one's pet dog.** Said when someone whom you trusted and supported most has betrayed you. Like nourishing a viper in your bosom and being harmed by it in the end.

近 bite the hand that feeds you; return evil for good; He has brought up a bird to pick out his own eyes.

25 蛙の子は蛙* 6級

日解與用法 とても**蛙の子**とは思えないおたまじゃくしだが、**成長すればやはり蛙**になるの意から、子の性質や能力は大抵親に似る。また、凡人の子は凡人にしかならないということの喩え。否定的な意味合いがある。

近義詞 この親にしてこの子あり 5級

漢 小蝌蚪長大是青蛙。子肖其父，什麼樣的父母必會有什麼樣的兒女。意指凡人之子難出英才，子輩多半步父母後塵。含貶義。

近 有其父必有其子；龍生龍、鳳生鳳，老鼠生的兒子會打洞；難窩裡飛不出金鳳凰；虎父無犬子

英 The child of a frog (tadpole) is still a frog. Fig. A son/daughter will have certain genetic traits from his/her father/mother upon reaching adulthood, both in behavior and physical characteristics. It usually has a negative connotation, since chilldren take after their parents.

近 Like father, like son.; Like breeds like.; (be a) chip off the old block; The apple does not fall far from the tree.

26 蛙の面に水* 6級

日解與用法 **蛙は顔に水をかけられても**けろりとしている。どんな仕打ちを受けても一向に動じない、何を言われてもしゃあしゃあとしている様子を言う。また、何の手ごたえのない事の喩え。

近義詞 牛の角を蜂が刺す 5級 石に灸 4級 蛙の面に小便 4級

漢 往青蛙臉上潑水。比喻無動於衷，打不知痛罵不知羞，絲毫不介意。

近 水澆鴨背；若無其事；滿不在乎

英 If you **splash water on the frog's face**, it doesn't upset the frog. Said about criticisms or insults won't affect someone at all.

近 like water off a duck's back

27 勝って兜の緒を締めよ* 6級

日解與用法 戦いに勝って、ほっと一息ついた時、不意に敵が襲ってくるとも限らないから、**勝ったとしても兜の紐を弛めず**、一層用心せよ。また、成功しても驕らず油断せず、さらに心を引き締めろという戒めの言葉。

近義詞 勝って驕らず 6級

漢 打贏仗後仍要繫緊頭盔的帶子，勿趾高氣揚。比喻勝不驕，維持高度警惕狀態。

近 勝而不驕；鞍不離馬，甲不離身

英 Fastening the strings of the helmet even after a victory. Don't exult too much but be sure not to rest on your arms and keep your guard up even after a victory; To take heed and keep your eye on the ball at all times.

近 Never halloo till you are out of the woods.; Do not sing your triumph before the victory.; Don't laugh when your enemy falls; don't crow over his collapse. (Bible)

28 亀の甲より年の功 ⑥級

日解與用法 **亀の甲羅より年寄りの貴重な経験。** 経験を積んだ年長者の知恵は亀卜（亀甲占い）より値打ちがあり、尊重すべきものだという喩え。古代の人々は亀の甲を焼いて現れたひびを見て吉凶・成敗を占った。

近義詞 医者と味噌は古いほどよい ④級　松笠より年嵩 ③級

漢 老人家的閱歷勝過烏龜的甲殼。年長者足智多謀，其智慧比龜卜有價值，提醒年輕人要懂得敬老尊賢。古代的人逢事必卜以推算吉凶成敗。

近 薑是老的辣；樹老根多，人老識多

英 **The efficacy of old age is better than the shell of a turtle.** "Age brings wisdom", "The older, the wiser". The advice of elderly people is more dependable than turtle-shell divination. Usually used as a reminder to young people to respect elderly people (Roasted turtle shells used to be used for fortune telling in ancient China).

近 They that live longest, see most.; Years know more than books.; Experience is the mother of wisdom.

29 枯れ木も山の賑わい* ⑥級

日解與用法 山を彩り、にぎやかな風情になるから、何もない殺風景なはげ山よりは**枯れ木でもあった方が**ましである。つまらないものも数に加えておけば、ないよりはあった方がいい。自分を謙遜して言う言葉なので、他人に対して使うのは失礼にあたる。

近義詞 餓鬼も人数 ③級

漢 即使枯樹也可增加山谷一些景色。比喻有總比沒有好。通常只用於自謙，形容說話者自己是混在集團中「濫竽充數」，但不宜用來形容別人。

近 聊勝於無；沒魚蝦也好

英 **Even withered trees liven up the hill.** Things of small worth are better than nothing. Usually used when someone said humbly that one's participation is just for adding to the total attendance at gathering (may sound a bit offensive against others, use it carefully).

近 It's better than nothing.; Half a loaf is better than none.; A bad bush is better than the open field.; The more, the merrier.

30 可愛い子には旅をさせよ* ⑥級

日解與用法 我が子が可愛いなら、親の元に置いて甘やかさずに、**旅に出して**世の中の辛さを体験させた方がよいということ。厳しい経験を積むほど成長するのだから、子供を敢えて厳しい環境におけという意。

近義詞 獅子の子落とし ⑤級

漢 疼愛子女要讓其出外旅遊，吃苦磨練。比喻教育子女須放手讓孩子學會自立更生，才會茁壯。

近 不打不成器；棍棒出孝子，嚴師出高徒；靜海造就不出好水手

英 **Sending a beloved child on a trip.** The notion that children will only grow up if disciplined, physically or mentally (traveling used to be a challenge which will enable youth to deal with all sorts of troubles).

近 Spare the rod and spoil the child.; Love well, whip well.

か行

17

31 雉も鳴かずば撃たれまい 6級

日解與用法 雉は鳴かなければ居所を知られず、猟師に撃たれることもなかった意。無用な発言が災いを招くので、口を慎めという戒めである。

近義詞 舌は禍の根 4級 三寸の舌に五尺の身を亡ぼす 4級

漢 野雞（綠雉）不叫就不會挨獵槍射擊。
比喻多話多惹禍，少出聲就沒事。

近 彈打出頭鳥，掌打多嘴人；是非只為
多開口（煩惱皆因強出頭）

英 The pheasant that keeps quiet is least likely to get shot. Said about someone who saves one's breath will trigger no harm. Watch what you say may keep you safe.

近 Silence seldom doth harm.; Don't speak unless you can improve on the silence.

32 臭い物に蓋 * 6級

日解與用法 悪臭が外に出ないように容器の蓋を閉める。不都合なことがよそへ漏れないように、よくない噂が立たないようにと、その場しのぎの手立てを講じることの喩え。

近義詞 ひた隠しにする 4級

漢 在發臭的東西上蓋蓋子。比喻刻意隱
瞞尷尬的事情或掩蓋醜聞，蒙混一時。

近 家醜不可外揚

英 Putting a lid over something that stinks. Fig. To attempt to hush up an disgraceful affair; To cover up what happened among the family members or the group one belongs to; To try to push a problem aside instead of dealing with it directly; To opt for a short-term solution when it demands immediate attention.

近 sweep the problem under the rug/carpet; Do not wash your dirty linen in public.; look the other way on 〜 ; turn a blind eye to 〜

33 腐っても鯛 * 6級

日解與用法 鯛は、鮮度が落ちて傷んでも高級魚であることに変わりはない。優れた人は落ちぶれても気品がある。素晴らしい物は悪い状態になっても、本来の価値を失わないということの喩え。

近義詞 千切れても錦 3級 沈丁花は枯れても芳し 3級

漢 即使不新鮮，鯛魚（加吉魚）還是鯛魚，
依舊值錢（在日本鯛魚屬於高級魚類）。
比喻傑出的人物再落魄起碼也不輸常
人，好貨儘管舊仍然勝於劣貨。

近 瘦死的駱駝比馬大；破雖破，蘇州貨；
爛船也有三斤釘；真金不怕火煉

英 Even though the sea bream has gone bad, it is still sea bream (considered a pricey fish in Japan). Fig. Thing of intrinsic value retains its brilliance regardless of the age. Brilliant people keep their quality no matter how their situation changes or however they may look.

近 A good horse becomes never a jade.; (A) diamond on a dunghill is a precious diamond still.

か行

34 犬猿の仲* 6級

日解與用法 仲が悪い喩えとして、**犬と猿の間柄**が挙げられる。犬と猿が出会えば、いがみ合うことから。しかし、日本の昔話『桃太郎』では、犬も猿も桃太郎に協力して鬼ヶ島の鬼を退治した、と語られている。

近義詞 水と油 6級　氷炭相容れず 3級

漢 彼此的關係像狗和猴子一樣不和睦，雙方一碰上就爭吵。比喻兩者無法和平相處。然而，童話『桃太郎』裏描述的小狗和小猴子是跟隨桃太郎前往鬼島為民除害。

近 水火不容；冰炭不同爐；貓鼠不同眠，虎鹿不同行

英 **Like the relationship between dogs and monkeys**, snarling at each other when bumping into one another. Said about people who don't get along well or don't really like each other. However, a dog and a monkey are known to help *Momotaro* (Peach Boy) to wipe out an orge in Japanese folklore.

近 Fight like cats and dogs.; on bad terms with 〜 ; at odds with each other

35 郷に入っては郷に従え 6級

日解與用法 知らない土地に行ったら、自分の価値観と異なっていても、**その土地の慣習や風俗にあった行動をとる**べきである。また、ある集団や組織に属した時は、その集団や組織の規律に従うのがよいということの喩え。

近義詞 門に入らば笠を脱げ 3級

漢 入鄉從鄉。比喻入境而問禁，入國而問俗。到一個地方，就依當地的習俗行事。

近 （入國問禁），入鄉隨俗

英 **When you get into a village, act the way that villagers are acting.** This phrase might come in handy when you're traveling abroad and notice that people around you do unfamiliar things. Follow the customs of the local people.

近 When in Rome do as the Romans do.

36 弘法にも筆の誤り* 6級

日解與用法 **弘法大師**のような書道の名人でも、**時には書き損じる**ことがある。どんな達人でも、時には失敗することがあるという喩え。

近義詞 猿も木から落ちる* 6級　竜馬の躓き 4級

漢 平安時代的大書法家弘法大師揮毫時偶而也會不小心寫錯。即使專家最拿手的事，也難保萬無一失。

近 善游者溺，善騎者墮；百密必有一疏，智者千慮，必有一失

英 **Even** the well-known monk, *Kōbō-Daishi* (also known as *Kūkai*, he is considered one of Japan's greatest calligraphers in the *Heian* Period) on occasion **makes an incorrect stroke** while writing in ink brush. Even someone who is the best at what they do can turn in a subpar performance. Everybody makes mistakes from time to time.

近 (Even) Homer sometimes nods.

19

37 五十歩百歩 ⑥級

日解與用法 戦場で**五十歩逃げた兵士が、百歩逃げた者を「臆病だ」と笑った**が、双方とも逃げたことには変わりはない。少しの差はあるものの、大きな違いはないことの喩え。中国語の成語に由来。

近義詞 目糞鼻糞を笑う ⑥級 　猿の尻笑い ④級

漢 逃了五十步的士兵譏笑另一個逃了一百步的士兵膽怯不中用。比喻譏笑別人，實際上自己亦半斤八兩，只是程度輕一點而已。

近 五十步笑百步；半斤八兩；烏鴉笑豬黑，龜笑鱉無尾

英 **One who retreats fifty paces mocks another who retreats a hundred** (borrowed from a Chinese proverb). A situation in which one person criticizes another for a fault or defect they have themselves. It makes no difference to each other.

近 The pot calling the kettle black.; six of one, half a dozen of the other

38 転ばぬ先の杖* ⑥級

日解與用法 **杖をついて歩けば、つまずいても転ばない。**転んでからでは遅い。万が一に備えて用心することが大切だということの喩え。

近義詞 備えあれば憂い無し* ⑥級 　濡れぬ先の傘 ⑤級

漢 未跌倒前手裏備好拐杖。凡事事先有準備，可免後患。穩妥總比後悔好。

近 未雨綢繆；有備無患；居安思危

英 **A walking stick lest you fall down.** Be prepared for anything. Take all necessary precautions. If you always are prepared, you can be rest assured of upcoming events. Better safe than sorry.

近 put something aside for a rainy day; Forewarned is forearmed.; Although the sun shines, leave not your cloak at home.

39 猿も木から落ちる* ⑥級

日解與用法 木登りに長けた**猿であっても、時には木から落ちる。**どんな名人も時には失敗することがあることの喩え。失敗を慰める言葉とも、油断を戒める言葉とも解することができる。

近義詞 河童の川流れ ⑥級 　上手の手から水が漏る ⑤級

漢 善爬樹的猴子，也有從樹上摔下來的時候。比喻再厲害的人偶爾也會失敗。

近 馬上摔死英雄漢，河中淹死會水人；人有失手，馬有亂蹄

英 **Even monkeys fall from trees.** Even skillful people mess up once in a while. No man is infallible.

近 The best cart may overthrow.; A good marksman may miss.; (A) horse may stumble though he has four legs.

20

40 触らぬ神に祟り無し＊ 6級

日解與用法 神とかかわりを持たなければ、神の祟りに遭わない。かかわり合いさえしなければ、災いを招くこともない、面倒なことに余計な手出しをするな、という戒め。祟りとは、神々が下した処罰（疫病、凶作、天災など）のこと。

近義詞 寝た子を起こすな 6級　触らぬ蜂は刺さぬ 4級　触り三百 3級

漢 不去冒犯神明就不會遭天譴。比喻勿惹是生非，別跟麻煩沾上關係，能免則免。

近 敬鬼神而遠之；多一事不如少一事；咎由自取

英 **Leave lesser gods alone to keep yourself out of divine retribution.** Said to keep someone or something at a respectful distance to avoid getting involved in problem, the less trouble the better. Keep your nose clean.

近 Let sleeping dogs lie.; Far from Jupiter far from thunder.

41 三人寄れば文殊の知恵＊ 6級

日解與用法 凡人でも三人集まって知恵を出し合えば、文殊菩薩のような良い知恵が出るものだということ。特別に利口な人でなくても三人集まって協力すれば何か良い考えが浮かぶものだ、という意。

近義詞 一人の好士より三人の愚者 3級

漢 三個平庸的人若同心協力集思廣益，也能擁有文殊菩薩（智慧之神）的智慧。意指集聚多人的智慧將會比一個聰明人還能想出好辦法來解決問題。

近 三個臭皮匠，勝過一個諸葛亮；人多出韓信，智多出孔明；一人計短，二人計長

英 **Three people equal in wisdom of Manjusri** (the Bodhisattva of Wisdom); Fig. Three ordinary people may be able to solve a problem quicker and better than a wise man working alone.

近 Two heads are better than one.; Four eyes see more than two.; So many heads, so many wits.

42 親しき仲にも礼儀あり＊ 6級

日解與用法 あまりにも親しみ過ぎて、遠慮がなくなると不和の元になる。どんなに親密な間柄でも節度を守ることが大切である、という意。

近義詞 親しき仲に垣をせよ 4級

漢 再親密也得顧及禮節。提醒人要有分寸，好朋友之間也要懂得尊重對方。人往往過分親近而不拘禮節，轉向輕侮對方。敬人者，人恆敬之。

近 親而不褻，近而不狎；相敬如賓；親兄弟明算帳

英 **Manners and courtesy are thought to be necessary even between close friends.** Friendship will flourish if you and your friend respect each other's privacy. A saying to remind people of knowing how close to intrude and when to stop.

近 Familiarity breeds contempt.; A hedge between keeps friendship green.; Love your neighbor, yet pull not down your hedge.

43 釈迦に説法 6級

日解與用法 仏教の開祖である**お釈迦さまに対して仏法を説く**。その道に精通している人に、その道を教えようとする愚かさを喩える。

近義詞 猿に木登り 5級　河童に水練 5級　孔子に論語 4級

漢 對佛祖釋迦牟尼講經，比喻在行家面前賣弄本領，不自量力。

近 班門弄斧；關公面前耍大刀

英 **A sermon to the Shakyamuni (Buddha).** Fig. Like teaching fish how to swim, teaching someone who is an expert in that area; To show off one's slight accomplishments in front of a specialist.

近 teach fish how to swim; preach to the converted/choir; teach one's grandmother to suck eggs

44 十人十色 6級

日解與用法 **十人いれば十種の色**(個性)がある。考え方、好みや性質などが人によってそれぞれに異なることの喩え。

近義詞 百人百様 5級　各人各様 4級

漢 十個人十種樣色。比喻人的想法・嗜好・個性不同。形形色色，各式各樣。

近 一龍生九種，種種各別；一種米養百種人

英 **Ten men, ten colors.** Fig. Everyone has his/her own ideas, tastes and personalities. Every person is entitled to his/her personal preferences. For example, something that one person considers boring or worthless may be considered interesting or valuable by someone else.

近 So many men, so many opinions/minds.; It takes all sorts to make a world.; One man's trash is another man's treasure.

45 朱に交われば赤くなる 6級

日解與用法 **朱色の辰砂に近づけば赤く染まってしまう**。付き合う人や環境によって、善悪いずれにも感化され、良くも悪くもなるということの喩え。

近義詞 麻の中の蓬 3級

漢 靠近朱砂的變紅。比喻接近好人可以使人變好，(接近壞人可以使人變壞)，比喻交友和環境對人影響很大。

近 近朱者赤，近墨者黑；挨金似金，挨玉似玉；蓬生麻中不扶而直

英 **One who mingles with vermilion turns red.** If you keep company with good people you will become good, and vice versa.

近 He that touches pitch shall be defiled.; Who keeps company with wolves, will learn to howl.; (A) man is known by the company he keeps.

46 知らぬが仏* 6級

日解與用法 事実を**知らないが**故に仏のように穏やかでいられること。知れば腹立たしいことも、知らなければ心を乱されずでいられるということの喩え。また、真相を知らず、のんきに構えている人を笑っても言う。

近義詞 聞くは気の毒、見るは目の毒 5級　見ぬもの清し 4級

漢 不知情者心靜如佛。比喻只要不知情或不在意，也就心平氣和不會為無謂之事生氣或煩惱。有時用於嘲弄被蒙在鼓裡的人。

近 眼不見為淨，耳不聽為清；眼不見心不煩

英 **Being left uninformed of something is blissful like Buddha.** One cannot be upset by something one does not know about. Possibly used as a cliché to tease a person who is kept in the dark.

近 Ignorance is bliss.; He that knows nothing, doubts nothing.; What the eye doesn't see, the heart doesn't grieve over.; Not knowing anything is the sweetest life. (Sophocles)

47 好きこそ物の上手なれ* 6級

日解與用法 **好きでやっていることは**一生懸命になるので、自然に**上達するもの**である。反対に、いやいややっているのでは、上手になれない、という。

近義詞 道は好むところによって安し 3級

漢 喜好的事就會駕輕就熟做得很好。所謂愛好促精通，即為此理。

近 知之者不如好之者，（好之者不如樂之者）

英 **One tends to do well what one likes,** fondness gives skill. Fig. A key to achieving excellence is to love what you do. In other words, people will not to be good at those things they dislike.

近 Who likes not his business, his business likes not him.

48 捨てる神あれば拾う神あり 6級

日解與用法 **見捨てる神もいれば**、一方で**助けてくれる神もいる**。見放す人がいる一方で、救いの手を差し伸べてくれる人もいるので、不運なことがあっても、悲観することはない、くよくよすることはないという喩え。

近義詞 地獄にも鬼ばかりはいない 4級

漢 有的神離棄你但也有的神幫助你。比喻人處困境時，上天總會給以出路的。

近 天無絕人之路；此處不留人，自有留人處

英 **While being deserted by one god, another god will give you a helping hand.** Fig. When someone deserts you, another will pick you up. When you lose one opportunity, you often find a different one comes to you. A cliché to encourage people never lose hope when beset with various problems.

近 When one door shuts, another opens.; When God closes a door, he opens a window.; God tempers the wind to the shorn lamb.

49 住めば都* 6級

日解與用法 どんな田舎であっても、どんなみすぼらしい環境であっても、**住み慣れれば都**と同じように住み心地がよくなるということの喩え。

近義詞 我が家楽の釜盥 4級　地獄も住み処 3級

漢 在一個地方住久後有了感情，再差的地方也感覺像住在京城一樣。意指沒有什麼地方比得上自己的家，久居則安。

近 金窩銀窩，不如自家的草窩

英 Where you live is a capital city (Fig. an attractive place). It implies that your own home is the most comfortable place to be, no matter where it is. Wherever one lives, one comes to love it.

近 There's no place like home.; East or west, home is best.; Every bird likes its own nest best.; Wherever I lay my hat is home.

50 急いては事を仕損じる* 6級

日解與用法 物事を**焦ってやると、失敗する**。急ぐ時ほど落ち着いて行動せよという戒め。

近義詞 急がば回れ* 6級　慌てる乞食は貰いが少ない 4級　急ぎの文は静かに書け 3級

漢 辦事過於性急圖快，難免有出錯。告誡人事情越急越需冷靜對應，凡事不可操之過急，倉促行事。

近 忙中有失；欲速則不達；慢工出細活；心急吃不了熱豆腐

英 If you make haste to complete something, you will make mistakes, you're likely to end up spending more time doing it. Don't rush because good and quickly seldom come together. A saying to remind people "Don't jump the gun", "Don't go off half-cocked". Plan out what you're going to do.

近 Haste makes waste.; More haste, less speed.; Soft fire makes sweet malt.; Haste is of the Devil. (St. Jerome)

51 船頭多くして船山に登る* 6級

日解與用法 船を操る**船頭さんが何人もいると、船の統制がとれなくなって山へ登ってしまう**。指図する人が多いと物事がうまく行かないという喩え。

近義詞 役人多くして事絶えず 4級

漢 操舵的人太多，最後船駛到山上去。比喻指使的人多而意見分歧，莫衷一是。結果成事不足敗事有餘。

近 艄公多了撐翻船；木匠多了蓋歪房；莫衷一是；成事不足敗事有餘

英 The boat with many coxswains will be driven up a mountain Fig. When there are too many people trying to manage something or give their opinions, they simply make a mess of it as it merely make things confusing.

近 Too many cooks spoil the broth.; Too many chiefs and not enough Indians.

52 備え有れば憂い無し＊ 6級

日解與用法 普段から万全の**備え(準備)**があれば、いざという時に何も**心配がない**ということ。

近義詞 転ばぬ先の杖＊ 6級

漢 凡事先做好一切準備，就不用擔憂。

近 有備無患；未雨綢繆；晴帶雨傘，飽帶飢糧；養兒防老，積穀防飢；養兵千日，用在一時

英 **Well prepared means no worries.** If you are always bracing yourself for a crunch, you'll be able to fall back on your reserves in case of emergency.

近 Keep your powder dry.; Forewarned is forearmed.; It is good to fear the worst; the best can save itself.; Prevention is better than cure.; Hope for the best and prepare for the worst.

53 損して得取れ＊ 6級

日解與用法 **少し損をして大きく儲けろ。**一時的に損をしても、将来大きな利益になって返ってくることを考えよということ。

近義詞 損は儲けの始め 4級　損せぬ人に儲けなし 4級

漢 先失後得，先賠後賺。暫時吃虧將來再伺機獲利，做事須從長遠打算。

近 吃小虧佔大便宜；放長線釣大魚；有失才有得

英 **To take profit from a loss.** Fig. To take a short term losses to realize a long term gains; To make a concession now for greater gain in the future; To make the best of a bad bargain.

近 Sometimes the best gain is to lose.; You must lose a fly to catch a trout.; A hook's well lost to catch a salmon.

54 立つ鳥跡を濁さず＊ 6級

日解與用法 **飛び立つ水鳥が水面を汚さないように、人も立ち去る時は、見苦しくないよう後始末をきちんとすべきであるという。**また、引き際は潔くしなければならないという戒めとしても使われる。

近義詞 飛ぶ鳥跡を濁さず 6級

漢 飛離的水鳥不汙穢水面。比喻人離開一個地方或工作單位時應該妥善地處理善後，不給別人留下麻煩，惹人非議。不給自己留下壞印象。

近 好聚好散；善始善終；好來不如好去；君子交絕，不出惡聲

英 **A bird does not pollute the water when taking wing.** Fig. Said that it is a common courtesy to clean up after oneself and end on a good note when resigning the group one belongs to.

近 Merry meet, merry part.; It's an ill bird that fouls its own nest.

55 立て板に水* [6級]

日解與用法 立てかけた板の上に水を一気に流すように、言葉がつかえることなく、すらすら話す様子をいう。弁舌が巧みで、よどみない流暢な話ぶりを喩える。

近義詞 舌が回る [6級] 弁が立つ [6級] 一瀉千里 [3級] 懸河の弁 [3級] 油紙へ火が付いたよう [3級] 竹に油を塗る [3級]

漢 像在豎板上澆水後，水傾瀉下來一樣。形容人能言善辯，十分健談。

近 口若懸河；滔滔不絕；連珠砲；三寸不爛之舌

英 To speak **like letting loose the water down to a standing board**; To reel something off and make people feel that it's hard to keep up with; Said about a person with a silver tongue, speaks with volubility.

近 talk a mile a minute; talk nineteen to the dozen

56 蓼食う虫も好き好き [6級]

日解與用法 辛味のある蓼を好んで食べる虫がいるように、人の好みも千差万別、多種多様である。人の好み・趣味について非難するのは愚かなことであるとほのめかしている。蓼は茎や葉に辛みがあり、香辛料として使われる。

近義詞 十人十色 [6級] 甲の薬は乙の毒 [4級]

漢 有些蟲偏愛有苦味的蓼葉；人各有所好，百人吃百味，不宜批評譏笑他人的嗜好。蓼是一種有苦味的草本植物，可食用。

近 青菜蘿蔔各有所好；麻油拌韭菜，各人心裏愛

英 **Some bugs prefer knotweed** (edible herb with a pungent flavor). Remarking about what is good or enjoyable for one person may not be so for someone else. There's no accounting for taste, therefore, we'd better not condemn people just because of what they like.

近 To each his own.; Every man to his taste.; Different strokes for different folks.; One man's meat is another man's poison.

57 棚から牡丹餅* [6級]

日解與用法 棚から落ちてきた牡丹餅が、ちょうど開いていた口の中に入る。努力せずして、思いがけない幸運が舞い込むことの喩え。略して「棚ぼた」。

近義詞 開いた口に牡丹餅 [4級] 鰯網へ鯛がかかる [3級]

漢 像櫥架上掉下來的豆沙餡餅，意指得來全不費工夫的意外收穫，若天賜之物。

近 喜從天降；福自天來；天落饅頭狗造化

英 **A sweet red bean rice cake from a shelf** (fall off the shelf right into someone's mouth). To have an unexpected and welcome luck; To receive a windfall. If something good falls into one's lap, it happens to him/her without any effort on his/her part.

近 pennies from heaven; manna from heaven

58 塵も積もれば山となる＊ 6級

日解與用法 塵のように小さなものでも、**積もり積もれば山のように大きくなる**ということ。どんなに小さなことでも、積み重ねればいつか大きなものになることの喩え。小さな事でもおろそかにしてはいけない教え。

近義詞 細き流れも大河となる 4級　砂長じて巌となる 3級

漢 積微塵而為山嶽，匯涓涓細流成大海；比喻聚少成多，任何事情都是日積月累，逐漸形成。亦提醒人即使微不足道的事物，也輕忽不得。

近 積土成山，（積水成淵）；聚沙成塔；集腋成裘

英 **Even piled-up specks of dust will accumulate to make a big mountain.** Said about little things which add up to bigger things. If you start with a little effort and continue to make an effort, you'll eventually achieve your goals. Do not underestimate small things.

近 Many a little makes a mickle.; Many drops make a shower.; Little and often fills the purse.; Every little bit helps.; A penny saved is a penny earned.

59 月と鼈＊ 6級

日解與用法 鼈は甲羅が丸く、俗に「まる」と異名で呼ばれる。月は満月で丸く見え、両者に共通しているのは形が丸いことだけ。本質的にはまったく違い、比較にならないほどかけ離れていることの喩え。

近義詞 提灯に釣鐘＊ 6級　雲泥の差 4級　下駄と焼き味噌＊ 4級

漢 月亮和鼈天差地遠，外形雖然都是圓形，但是月亮高掛在夜空，很美。而鼈棲在泥塘裏，很醜。比喻相差懸殊，不能相提並論。

近 天壤之別；雲泥之別；天懸地隔；大相逕庭

英 **As different as the moon from soft-shell turtle**, even though they both look roughly circular in shape. A cliché used to suggest that two people or things, superficially alike, are totally different from each other in their other qualities.

近 different as chalk and cheese; different as night and day

60 鶴の一声 小6級

日解與用法 瑞鳥である**鶴の**甲高い**声**。権威ある者や有力者の、衆人を従わせるような一声で事が決まるということの喩え。

近義詞 雀の千声、鶴の一声 5級

漢 鶴唳一聲。指有影響力有權勢者說話有份量，往往憑一句話就能定局，就可排除眾議解決問題。

英 **A single cry of a crane.** A figurative expression of the voice made by a figure of authority or the final top-down decision; One word from a wise man carries enormous weight.

近 一言九鼎；一鳥入林，百鳥壓音；一錘定音；登高一呼

近 have the last word; A king's word was more than another man's oath.

27

61 鉄は熱いうちに打て * 6級

日解與用法 鉄は熱して軟らかいうちに打つように、①人は若いうちに教育して鍛えることが大事だという教え。②物事を行うにはタイミングを逃してはならない、という意でも使う。英語の言い回しに由来 (英語の句は後者の意味のみ)。

近義詞 矯めるなら若木のうち 4級　好機逸すべからず 4級

漢 打鐵趁熱。日語除②勿坐失良機以外，亦有①教育必須從小開始鍛鍊的意思。

近 ①教兒趁小，(扶木趁嫩)　②打鐵趁熱

英 Strike while the iron is hot (borrowed from an English proverb). However, in Japanese, there're two meanings: ① To educate kids when they can learn is like bending a young twig ② To act at the best possible time; To take advantage of favorable conditions.

近 ① As the twig is bent, so is the tree inclined. ② Strike while the iron is hot.; Make hay while the sun shines.; not let the grass grow under your feet

62 出る杭は打たれる * 6級

日解與用法 並べた杭が一本だけ高ければ、他の杭と揃うように打たれることから、才能があってぬきんでている者は、とかく人から憎まれる。また、差し出たことをする者は、人から非難され、制裁を受ける。

近義詞 高木は風に折らる 4級

漢 突出的木樁先被人鎚。比喻才華出眾的人易討人嫌，或鋒芒畢露好出風頭的人易被攻擊。

近 出頭的椽子先爛；棒打出頭鳥；樹大招風；人怕出名豬怕肥

英 The nail that pops up gets hammered down; Fig. If you excel or succeed, you are subject to criticism. People tend to evoke a feeling of jealousy or criticise someone who stands out from the crowd. One who pushes oneself forward or keeps a high profile will be knocked down by peers.

近 cut down the tall poppies (tall poppy syndrome); Tall trees catch much wind.

63 灯台下暗し * 6級

日解與用法 燭台は周囲を明るく照らすが、その真下には光が届かず暗いことから、人は身近なことには案外気がつかないものだという喩え。

近義詞 負うた子を三年探す 4級　近くて見えぬは睫 3級

漢 蠟燭可以照亮四周但照不到燭台正方，因此燭台底下反而最暗。引申為雖近卻反而看不見，人往往對身邊的事物視而不見。

近 丈八燈臺照遠不照近；騎驢找驢；騎牛找牛

英 It is dark at the foot of the candlestick because the candle sheds light on all around but right under it. Said that it's hard to see from what is right under your nose.

近 The darkest place is under the candlestick.; Go abroad and you'll hear news of home; You must go into the country to hear what news at London.; No one may be a judge in his own cause.

28

64 捕らぬ狸の皮算用* 6級

日解與用法 狸を捕まえないうちに皮を売って儲ける計算をする意から、まだ手に入るかどうかも分からない不確かなものを当てにして、ああだこうだと計画を練ることの喩え。

近義詞 飛ぶ鳥の献立 4級　儲けぬ前の胸算用 4級

漢 沒抓到狐狸就數皮件。提醒人勿謀之過早，勿操之過急，如意算盤別打得太早。

近 還沒打著狗熊，先別說分皮的話

英 **Counting the skins of raccoon dogs which not yet been caught.** Said to remind someone don't be too confident in expecting good fortune before it is certain.

近 Don't count your chickens before they are hatched.; Catch your bear before you sell its skin.; First catch your hare, then cook him. ; Never spend your money before you have it.

65 団栗の背比べ 6級

日解與用法 どんぐりは形も大きさもほぼ一様で差がないので、背比べをしても大して違わない。どれもこれも似たり寄ったりで、特に目立つものがないことの喩え。

近義詞 一寸法師の背比べ 4級　どっこいどっこい

漢 橡實比大小。橡實形狀大小其實都差不多。比喻平庸無奇的東西分不出高低好壞，拿來比大小毫無意義。

近 不相上下；半斤八兩；伯仲之間

英 **Acorns compare their height with each other.** Competition among the mediocre. Fig. There is little difference between two choices that have no particularly outstanding characteristics. Alludes to a bragging contest as a matter of little importance.

近 Never a barrel the better herring.; tweedledum and tweedledee; much of a muchness

66 飛んで火に入る夏の虫* 6級

日解與用法 灯火を目がけて飛んでくる夏の羽虫のように、自ら進んで危険や災難に身を投げる無謀な行動を笑って言う。

近義詞 手を出して火傷する 4級

漢 飛蛾撲到火焰上。比喻魯莽，不考慮後果的行為，自取滅亡。

近 飛蛾撲火（自尋死路）；自投羅網

英 **Like summer insects (such as moths) that fly into a flame.** A figurative expression of a reckless person who rides for a fall and precipitate one's ruin. Be doomed to extinction.

近 The fly flutters about the candle till at last it gets burnt.; Fools rush in where angels fear to tread.

67 長い物には巻かれろ 6級

日解與用法 **長い物には巻かれる**方が無難である。目上の者や、自分の手に負えないほどの権力を持つ相手には逆らわず、大人しく従う方が利口だという喩え。

近義詞 泣く子と地頭には勝てぬ* 5級 時の代官、日の奉行 3級

漢 面對**長**的東西時就任它去捲吧！意指弱小的力量敵不過強大的勢力。面對長輩或有權勢的人，最好邊就其意委曲求全。既在矮簷下，怎敢不低頭？

近 胳膊扭不過大腿；勿以螳臂擋車；勿以卵擊石

英 **Better be looped around by something long** (Fig. a person with power). It's no use kicking against the pricks. If you can't defeat the people in power, you might be better off by switching to their side.

近 If you can't beat them, join them!; You can't fight City Hall.; Better bend than break.; If the master says the crow is white, the servant must not say 'tis black.

68 泣き面に蜂* 6級

日解與用法 **泣いている人の顔を蜂が刺す。**苦痛の上にさらに苦痛が重なる、また、不運の上に災難が重なることの喩え。

近義詞 弱り目に祟り目 6級 踏んだり蹴ったり 6級 傷口に塩 5級

漢 流著眼淚的臉又被蜜蜂螫到。比喻不幸的事接二連三地發生，使傷害更嚴重。

近 禍不單行；屋漏偏逢連夜雨，船遲又遇打頭風；雪上加霜

英 **Have a bee sting on one's tear-stained face.** A figurative expression that bad things always come in groups, they never come alone.

近 Misfortunes never come singly.; When it rains, it pours.; Bad things come in threes.; add insult to injury; rub salt in wounds

69 情けは人の為ならず* 6級

日解與用法 **情けをかけるということは、他人のためばかりでなく、自分のためだ。**他人に親切にしておけば、いずれその報いが巡り巡って自分に返ってくるのであるから、人には親切にせよという教え。

近義詞 積善の家には必ず余慶あり 3級

漢 行善並非只為別人，而是為自己。意指若關懷憐憫別人，改天也許會得到相同的回報。

近 與人方便，自己方便；善有善報；積善之家必有餘慶

英 **Mercy or compassion is not only for the sake of others.** Fig. Kindness comes back like a boomerang to those who are kind. It means a favor should be repaid with another favor. The good you do for others is good you do for yourself.

近 Kindness begets kindness.; One good turn deserves another.; The hand that gives gathers.; What goes around, comes around.

な行

70 七転び八起き* 6級

日解與用法 七度転んで八度起き上がる。困難に見舞われても立ち上がり、失敗を繰り返しても挫けず、頑張り通すことの喩え。また、浮き沈みの激しい人生を喩える。

近義詞 七転八起 4級

漢 跌了七次爬起八次。比喻歷經幾番挫折毫不退縮，仍然繼續努力。或意指盛衰起伏不定，榮枯無常的人生。

近 百折不撓；不屈不撓；再接再厲

英 Fall down seven times and get back on one's feet eight times. Fig. Standing up again after repeated failures. The wheel of life keeps on turning. Never yield in spite of all setbacks. Also used as an implication of ups and downs in life.

近 If at first you don't succeed, try, try again.; He that falls today may be up again tomorrow.

71 習うより慣れよ* 6級

日解與用法 物事は、人や本に**教わる**よりも、自分が実際に体験して**慣れ親しんだ**方が、よく覚えられ、身につくということ。

近義詞 経験は学問にまさる 4級　経験は愚か者の師 3級

漢 理論上的**學習不如**實際上的**適應**，熟練了才能找到竅門而得心應手。請教別人或擁有書本知識不如身體力行。

近 熟能生巧；一遍生，二遍熟

英 Better to become experienced than to be taught. Skill comes from practice. Fig. If you do something many times you will get the hang of it; Possibly implying "practical knowledge rather than book knowledge".

近 Practice makes perfect.; Custom makes all things easy.; Wit once bought is worth twice taught.

72 二階から目薬* 6級

日解與用法 二階から階下にいる人に**目薬**をさしても目に入らない。思うようにならなくて歯がゆい、また、回りくどくて効果のないことを指す。

近義詞 靴を隔てて痒きを掻く 5級　遠火で手を焙ぶる 3級

漢 從二樓（給樓下的人）點眼藥。引申為力不從心，因起不了作用而感到焦躁，或比喻因方法不直截而毫無效益。

近 隔靴搔癢；徒勞無功；遠水不救近火；遠水不解近渴

英 Eye-drops from upstairs. Fig. To fail to get at the seat of the trouble. Something that cannot work no matter how hard one tries (and is quite frustrating because of an ineffective and circuitous approach). Similar to an itchy spot which is just out of reach.

近 strive in vain; (be) of no avail / without any avail

な行

73 二兎を追う者は一兎をも得ず* 6級

日解與用法 二羽の兎を一度に捕らえようとしても一羽も捕まえることができない。同時に二つの事をしようとすれば、結局どちらも成功しないという喩え。

近義詞 虻蜂取らず 6級　欲の熊鷹股裂くる 3級

漢 逐二兔者不得其一。比喻一心兩用的人，一事無成。

近 腳踏兩條船，必定落空；飛了鴨子打了蛋，兩頭落空

英 He who hunts two hares will not catch either. Fig. A caution that you cannot do two things successfully at the same time.

近 If you run after two hares, you will catch neither.; Between two stools one falls to the ground.; (A) man cannot whistle and drink at the same time.

74 猫に小判* 6級

日解與用法 小判とは、江戸時代に流通した金貨の一種である。猫は小判の価値が分からないので、小判をもらっても何の反応もしない。転じて、値打ちのある貴重なものでも、持つ人によって何の役にも立たないことをいう。

近義詞 豚に真珠 6級

漢 給貓兒「小判」（江戶時代的貨幣）。比喻把珍貴的東西給有眼無珠的人，不知賞識，毫無意義，白費心機。

近 明珠暗投

英 Give "koban" (an old Japanese coin used during Edo period) to a cat. Fig. For someone who has no interest in something even valuable, giving him or her it would not be appreciated. Possibly be interpreted when giving someone a nice thing which he/she doesn't deserve.

近 cast pearls before swine (Bible)

75 猫の手も借りたい* 6級

日解與用法 鼠を捕ること以外、何の役にも立たない猫の手であっても、その手を借りたいと思うほど、休む暇もなく非常に忙しい。書き入れ時のように、誰でもいいから手伝いが欲しい時に用いる表現。

近義詞 犬の手も人の手にしたい 3級

漢 忙碌的連貓的手都得借來幫忙。比喻工作太多，十分忙亂而人手不足。

近 忙得焦頭爛額；忙得不可開交；忙得腳不沾地

英 To want to borrow even a cat's paw, be extremely busy or be severely understaffed due to insufficient workforce so that even a cat's "hand" would help. Fig. When someone is in desperate need of a helping hand, any help would be appreciated.

近 need an extra pair of hands; up to one's neck/ears/eyes/eyeballs (in work)

な行

32

76 寝耳に水* ⁶級

日解與用法 眠っている時に耳に水が入るような、思いがけない出来事や知らせに驚くこと、出し抜けにびっくりさせられることの喩え。

近義詞 青天の霹靂 ⁶級　藪から棒* ⁶級　足下から鳥が立つ ⁴級

漢 像正在睡覺的時候耳朵進水一樣。比喻對突如其來的事端或出乎意料的消息感到震驚。

近 晴天霹靂

英 **Like cold water into someone's ears while sleeping**, refers to the unlikelihood of an event. Said when news came as a big surprise or shock to someone and upset them very much. Like someone drops a bombshell on you.

近 (a) bolt from the blue / out of the blue

---

77 念には念を入れよ* ⁶級

日解與用法 「念を入れる」とは細かい点にまで注意する意。気をつける上にも、さらに注意を重ねよ、という強調の言葉。

近義詞 石橋を叩いて渡る ⁶級　浅い川も深く渡れ ⁴級

漢 注意再注意。倍加小心，再三留意。

近 小心謹慎；吃飯防噎，走路防跌

英 **Cannot be too careful.** ; To err on the side of caution. Fig. Something that you say in order to advise someone to think about possible problems and make assurance double sure.

近 Measure twice and cut once.; It is best to be on the safe side.; Hear twice before you speak once.; wear both belt and braces

---

78 能ある鷹は爪を隠す* ⁶級

日解與用法 有能な鷹は獲物にみすかされないように、鋭い爪を隠しておくことから、才能や実力の持ち主は、軽々しくそれをひけらかすことはしないという喩え。

近義詞 深い川は静かに流れる ³級　鳴かない猫は鼠捕る ³級

漢 有能力的老鷹把爪子藏起來。比喻大智若愚，有真材實學的人不展才，不露鋒芒，不四處炫耀自己。

近 真人不露相；會捉老鼠的貓不叫；虎豹不外其爪，而噬不見齒；韜光養晦

英 **A clever hawk hides its talons.** Fig. A wise man hides one's light under a bushel or keeps one's cards close to one's chest. One who does not talk very much and show off one's knowledge.

近 Still waters run deep.; Who knows most speaks least.; (A) still tongue makes a wise head.; Greatest genius often lies concealed.

な行

79 花より団子* 6級

日解與用法 花より団子の方がよい。桜の花を眺めて目を楽しませるより団子を食べて食欲を満たした方がよいの意から、風流よりは実利、外観よりは中身を重んじるということの喩え。また、風雅を解さない人を茶化す表現として使う。

近義詞 色気より食い気 4級　名を捨てて実を取る 3級　花の下より鼻の下 3級

漢 賞櫻花不如吃糯米丸子。比喻不愛風流愛實惠，也用來奚落不懂風雅的人。

近 捨華求實

英 **Prefer dumplings to flowers.** The idea that people tend to be more interested in food than in cherry-blossoms. Fig. The practical over the aesthetic; substance over style. Also used as a common taunt to tease people who are pragmatic about everything.

近 Bread is better than the songs of birds.; Better fill a glutton's belly than his eye.

80 歯に衣着せぬ 6級

日解與用法 歯に布を被せない。つまり、相手に遠慮せず、思った事を包み隠さずに言う。へつらわずに、思ったとおりをずけずけと言うことの喩え。

近義詞 単刀直入 5級　忌憚無く言う

漢 不單布塊在牙齒上。比喻有話據實以告，不拐彎抹角。說話乾脆，直截了當。

近 直言不諱；單刀直入；打開天窗說亮話

英 **Not to overlay teeth with cloth.** Fig. To speak frankly; To speak straight from the shoulder, even if it is impolite; To tell it like it is no matter how unpleasant or how much it hurts.

近 call a spade a spade; mince no words; (not to) beat around the bush

81 人の振り見て我が振り直せ* 6級

日解與用法 人の行動を見て、自分の行いを改めよという。つまり、他人の行動の良い所は見習い、悪い所についてはそうするな、と自分に言い聞かせる。

近義詞 他山の石、以て玉を攻むべし 5級　殷鑑遠からず 4級　前車の覆るは後車の戒め 4級　人こそ人の鏡 3級

漢 看別人的行為修正自己的行為。借鏡他人的行為學得教訓，取其長處幫助自己學習，察其短處警惕自己。

近 三人行，必有我師焉；他山之石，可以攻玉；以銅為鏡，可以正衣冠；以人為鏡，可以知得失；殷鑑不遠；前車之鑑

英 **Look at the manners of others and mend your own.** Fig. By observing other's faults wise men correct their own. One man's fault is another's lesson. There is always someone to learn from.

近 Wise men learn by other men's mistakes.

82 百聞は一見に如かず* 6級

日解與用法 人の話を百回聞いても、自分の目で直接一度見ることに及ばない。実際に自分の目で見れば、理解し納得が行くということの喩え。中国の成語に由来。

近義詞 論より証拠* 6級

漢 聽百遍不如親眼看一遍。聽別人述說多次，不如親眼看一次來得真確可信。意指口說不如身逢，耳聞不如目睹。

英 **One real witness is better than hundred hearsays** (borrowed from a Chinese expression). You need to see something yourself to believe it or to dispel any doubts. Visualisation is generally better than a verbal description.

近 百聞不如一見；耳聽為虛，眼見為實

近 Seeing is believing.; (A) picture is worth a thousand words.; Better one eye-witness than two hear-say witnesses.

83 瓢箪から駒* 6級

日解與用法 瓢箪の細い口から、馬が飛び出す意から、意外なところから、思いも寄らないものが出てくることや、ふざけ半分の事柄が実現してしまうことをいう。また、あるはずのないことが現実になることの喩え。

近義詞 嘘から出た真* 6級 灰吹きから蛇が出る 4級

漢 葫蘆裡跑出駿馬。比喻意料不到或不可能發生的事情居然成為事實。也比喻有口無心地戲言成為事實。

英 **Pony pops out of a gourd** beyond expectation. Fig. Something said as a joke that actually happened later. An unanticipated things or impossible things which happen to one's surprise.

近 事出意外；弄假成真 / 戲言成真

近 Mows may come to earnest.; Many a true word is spoken in jest.

84 豚に真珠 6級

日解與用法 豚に真珠を与える。豚はその価値を知らないことから、どんな立派なものでも、その値打ちを知らない者にとっては無価値に等しく、なんの役にも立たないものである。新約聖書に由来する表現。

近義詞 猫に小判* 6級 犬に論語 4級

漢 **投珠與豚**。意指把珍貴的東西給不識貨的人，白白糟蹋它毫無意義。源自聖經新約全書。

英 **Casting pearls before swine.** Giving something valuable to someone who does not understand that it is precious (comes from the Bible).

近 明珠暗投；對牛彈琴

近 cast pearls before swine (Bible)

は行

35

85 坊主憎けりゃ袈裟まで憎い 6級

日解與用法 坊さんを憎むと、坊さんが着ている袈裟までが憎たらしくなる。その人を憎むあまり、その人に関わるすべてのものが憎くなることの喩え。逆に、「愛、屋烏に及ぶ 3級」は、人を愛するとその家の屋根に止まっている烏まで好きになってしまうという意味。

近義詞 親が憎けりゃ子も憎い 3級

漢 若覺得和尚可憎,連和尚穿的袈裟(法衣)都討厭。比喻憎恨一個人,連其周遭所有人‧事物都看不順眼。相反的現象就是所謂的「愛屋及烏」。

近 憎人及物;愛之欲其生,惡之欲其死;愛之深,責之切

英 **He who hates a monk hates even his robe.** Said that people tend to detest everything that's associated with someone who bear a grudge against. In contrast, "Love me, love my dog".

近 We hate our enemy and the ground he walks on. ; He who hates Peter harms his dog.; hate someone's guts

86 仏の顔も三度* 6級

日解與用法 慈悲深い仏様といえども、三度も顔を撫で回されたら腹を立てるということ。どんなに温厚な人でも、何度も無礼をされれば、しまいには怒り出すという喩え。

近義詞 堪忍袋の緒が切れる 5級　兎も七日なぶれば噛み付く 3級

漢 即使是佛陀,若臉孔被他人亂摸三次也會動怒的。比喻容忍有限,個性再溫順的人若老是受欺負也會大發雷霆的。

近 事不過三;忍無可忍

英 **Even the Buddha** will get angry **when people touch his face for the third time.** Fig. Even a person who seems to have the patience of a saint and never allow anything to upset him/her, has a limit. If you've tried his/her patience too far, they will hit the ceiling.

近 Beware the fury of a patient man.; Patience has its limits.

87 負けるが勝ち* 6級

日解與用法 相手を立てて自分の勝ちに繋げる。強いて争わないで相手に勝ちを譲った方が、自分に有利な結果をもたらすことになる。無駄な争いを避けろという教え。また、負けた人を慰める言葉としても使われる。

近義詞 逃げるが勝ち 4級　花を持たせる 4級

漢 以輸為贏。引申為勿硬與他人爭奪眼前一時的勝利,表面上退讓一步輸給對方,實際上自己才是最終的贏家。或指讓一寸,鏡一尺,雖敗猶榮,改天才有贏的機會。

近 敗中求勝;以退為進;讓禮一寸,得禮一尺

英 **To lose is to win, by yielding one survives.** Said when you think that sometimes when you lose, you really win because yielding is sometimes the best way of succeeding, it is assumed that by such a move you live to fight another day.

近 stoop to conquer; The cheerful loser is the winner.; One pair of heels is often worth two pairs of hands.

88 馬子にも衣装（衣裳） * 6級

日解與用法 「馬子（馬方）」は江戸時代、馬を引いて荷物を運ぶことを職業とする人。その**馬子でも見栄えのする衣装を着せて**やれば格好よく見える。身なりを整えれば、どんな人でも立派に見えることの喩え。

近義詞 公家にも襤褸 ③級 鬼瓦にも化粧 ③級 浮世は衣装七分 ③級

漢 即使馬夫只要衣冠楚楚，風貌就不同。比喻體面氣派需要靠衣著裝扮，強調穿著可建立形象亦增加風采。

近 人要衣裳，佛要金裝；人靠衣裝，馬靠鞍

英 **Even a packhorse driver would look good in nice clothes.** Said that fine clothes may make the wearer seem more impressive than he or she really is; Anyone can look good if he or she is well-dressed.

近 Fine feathers make fine birds.; The tailor makes the man.; Clothes make the man.

89 待てば海路の日和あり 6級

日解與用法 海が荒れても、**じっと待っていれば、やがては出航にふさわしい良い天気になる。**焦らずに待っていればチャンスはそのうちにやってくるということの喩え。

近義詞 果報は寝て待て * 6級 待てば甘露の日和あり * 4級

漢 壞天氣時的航海須靜待天氣轉晴。比喻凡事只要耐心等待，時機終會到來，運氣終會轉好。意即成功屬於耐心等待的人。

近 守得雲開見月明；時來運轉；蓄勢待發

英 **Fine weather will come for your safe voyage if you wait.** An expression to encourage people if they are prepared to wait patiently, they usually get what they want in the end.

近 Everything comes to him who waits.; It is a long lane that has no turning.

90 身から出た錆 * 6級

日解與用法 **刀身から出た錆が、刀身を腐らせて**しまう。自分の悪い行いが原因で、苦しんだり災いに遭ったりすることの喩え。

近義詞 自業自得 6級 因果応報 6級 悪事身に返る ③級

漢 從刀身跑出來的鐵鏽。比喻做壞事的人遲早會得到報應，咎由自取、罪有應得。

近 自食惡果；自作自受；作繭自縛；腳上泡自己走的

英 **The rust comes from the blade** itself. Fig. The problem of one's own making; Said that one would pay for one's past mistakes or suffer the consequences of one's bad deeds.

近 get one's just deserts; face the music; fry in one's own grease; stew in one's own juice

91 三つ子の魂百まで* 6級

日解與用法 三歳児の魂は百歳になっても変わらない。つまり、幼児期に形成された性格や性質は一生変わるものではない。

近義詞 雀百まで踊り忘れず* 6級　噛む馬はしまいまで噛む 3級

漢 三歳孩子的裏性到百歲（也不會改變）。比喻幼時的性格氣質長大後也改不了。

近 三歲定八十；狗改不了吃屎；江山易改，本性難移；牛牽到北京也是牛

英 **The spirit of a child of three will stay unchanged until a hundred.** Fig. A person cannot change his/her basic character or quality once it has been formed in early childhood. An influence on a person as a child will remain unchanged through life.

近 The child is father of the man./The child is father to the man.; A leopard doesn't change its spots.; The fox may grow grey, but never good.; What's bred in the bone will come out in the flesh.

92 目から鱗が落ちる 6級

日解與用法 鱗で目を塞がれて見えなかったものが、その鱗が落ちて見えるようになること。あることがきっかけで、それまで分からなかった本質や事態が急に理解・認識できるようになることを喩える。新約聖書に由来。

近義詞 目が洗われる 4級

漢 眼上的鱗片掉下來。比喻因某種契機突然領悟開竅，明白某個道理。源自聖經新約全書。

近 茅塞頓開；恍然大悟

英 **The scales fall from eyes.** Said that someone is suddenly awakened to the truth or has an "aha" moment from a solution to a problem. This saying comes from the Christian Bible.

近 The scales fall from one's eyes.; see the light

93 餅は餅屋* 6級

日解與用法 餅は餅屋の搗いたものが一番美味しいということ。何事においてもその道の専門家に任せるのが一番良いということの喩え。また、上手とは言え素人では専門家にかなわないということの喩え。

近義詞 蛇の道は蛇 5級　馬は馬方 3級　芸は道によって賢し 3級　海の事は舟子に問え、山の事は樵夫に問え 3級

漢 麻糬還是麻糬店舖的好吃。比喻辦事須找內行專家才確實可靠，行行有竅門。或形容即使本事還是差專家半截。

近 隔行如隔山；術業有專攻

英 **Go to the rice cake maker to get a delicious one.** Said that you should go to specialists for the best results because every man knows his own business best. Carrying a connotation of "you have a ways to go to catch up with a professional, though you are fairly good now".

近 Horses for courses.; There are tricks in every trade.

ま行

94 門前の小僧習わぬ経を読む＊ 6級

日解與用法 寺の**門前に**住む子供は読経を聞くうちに**習わないお経も唱えられる**ようになる。日頃から見たり聞いたりしているものは、知らず知らずのうちに覚えてしまう。人は環境に強く影響されることの喩え。

近義詞 勧学院の雀は蒙求を囀る 3級

漢 居住在廟前的兒童，不學就會唸經。比喻經常耳聽眼看，不知不覺地受到影響，無師自通。意指周圍的環境對人的影響很大。

近 耳濡目染；潛移默化

英 **A boy living near the gate of a temple recites sutras he has never learned.** Fig. To learn something by heart spontaneously; To pick up certain things unconsciously when you're exposed to it daily, implying people are prone to be influenced by their surroundings.

近 A saint's maid quotes Latin.

95 焼け石に水＊ 6級

日解與用法 **焼けて**熱くなった**石に少しの水を**かけてもすぐに蒸発してしまい、容易には冷めない。僅かばかりの努力や援助では、何の効果もないことの喩え。

近義詞 大海の一滴 4級　九牛の一毛に過ぎない 4級

漢 用一點水潑在熱石頭上，立刻蒸發掉。比喻力量渺小，或指資助微不足道，無濟於事。

近 杯水車薪；滄海一粟

英 **Like trying to cool a hot stone with a couple of drops of water**, evaporates instantly. Said about an utterly inadequate attempt or assistance which is not enough to save the situation.

近 like a drop in a bucket; hardly make a dent in ～；What is a pound of butter among a kennel of hounds?

96 安物買いの銭失い＊ 6級

日解與用法 **値段が安いものは**品質が悪いので、買い得と思っても結局は修理や買い替えで**損をしてしまう。**

近義詞 一文惜しみの百損 4級　安かろう悪かろう 5級

漢 買便宜貨賠錢。便宜貨往往品質差，不是修理就是替換，容易吃暗虧。比喻貪圖廉價品便宜反而增加花費。

近 貪賤買老牛，（一年倒三頭）；貪小失大；一分錢，一分貨

英 **A waste of money on cheap goods.** Said that things which are obtained cheaply often end up exacting the heaviest prices. The quality of a good increases as its price increases.

近 You get what you pay for.; Cheapest is dearest.; Ill ware is never cheap.; A thing you don't want is dear at any price.

や行

97 油断大敵* 6級

日解與用法 たいしたことはないだろうと**気が緩むと、思わぬ失敗を招く。**不注意が何よりも恐れるべき敵だという。注意を怠るな、気の弛みを戒めた言葉。

近義詞 油断は不覚の基 4級

漢 掉以輕心是大敵（大害）。比喻處理事情時切忌抱著輕忽或漫不經心的態度，容易招致功虧一簣。

近 小心駛得萬年船；大意失荊州

英 **Carelessness is a great enemy.** Said to mean that a person who doesn't give due care and attention lies at the root of failure. There's many a slip twixt cup and lip, it'll be safe and sound as long as you don't let your guard down.

近 Danger comes soonest when it is despised.; The way to be safe is never to feel secure.; Security is mortals' greatest enemy.

98 良薬口に苦し* 6級

日解與用法 **効く薬は苦くて飲みにくい。**身のためになる忠告は厳しく聞こえ、素直に受け入れにくいということの喩え。中国の成語に由来。

近義詞 忠言耳に逆らう 5級

漢 好的藥往往味苦難吃。比喻衷心的勸告或批評，往往聽起來覺得嚴厲刺耳，但對聽者是有益的。

近 良藥苦口（忠言逆耳）

英 **A good medicine tastes bad in the mouth** (borrowed from a Chinese proverb). Fig. To find honest advice distasteful. Frank criticism may sound harsh to the ears (hard to take).

近 Bitter pills may have wholesome effects.; Advice when most needed is least heeded.

99 類は友を呼ぶ* 6級

日解與用法 **同じ種類の人が寄り集まる。**気の合った者や似通った者同士は、自然に寄り集まって仲間を作るようになる。

近義詞 類を以て集まる* 4級　同類相求む 3級　牛は牛連れ、馬は馬連れ* 3級

漢 同類的人會呼朋引伴。比喻性質志趣相近的人相互招引，自然地聚集在一起。

近 物以類聚，人以群分；方以類聚，物以群分；同聲相應，同氣相求；聲應氣求

英 **People of the same type tend to associate with each other.** Fig. People who have similar characters or similar interests often choose to spend time together.

近 Birds of a feather flock together.; Like attracts like.; Like will to like.

ら行

100 渡る世間に鬼はない ^{6級}

日解與用法 冷たい世の中に見えるが、鬼のように無慈悲な人ばかりではなく、親切で人情に厚い人もいる、困れば助けてくれる心優しい人もいるという。

近義詞 地獄にも仏あり ^{4級}

漢 人世間無惡鬼。比喻人世間並非都是冷淡無情的人，遇到困難時也總會有好人幫助你。

近 人間處處有溫情；冷暖人間

英 There is no real orge in the world. In other words, reality is not as cruel as you may think, there are people ready to lend a hand everywhere. All humans are somewhat kind at heart.

近 There is kindness to be found everywhere.; Love will creep where it may not go.

コラム1

幕末 『狂斎百図』 河鍋暁斎画
時田昌瑞ことわざコレクション 明治大学博物館所蔵

当初はバラで売られていたようだが、後に色々な体裁で発行されたり、再版や一枚の刷り物にされたり、絵葉書などにも転用されたくらいに人気があった。題名には百とあるが、実際は百以上ある。激烈な色づかいとなっている特色がある。暁斎もことわざに関心が高かったようで、他に肉筆画も何種類も描いている。

わ行

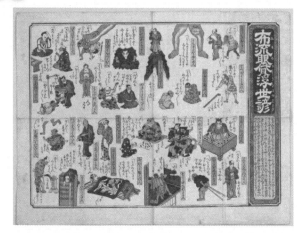

江戸後期 『布流眼貸浮世諺』 作者不詳
時田昌瑞ことわざコレクション 明治大学博物館所蔵

一枚刷りのことわざ尽くしの早い時期に発行されたものと推定される。23のことわざとその絵を一枚にしている。同趣向のものの中では用紙ともども最大のもの。

コラム3

江戸後期から発行された「ことわざ尽くし」の一種。現在まで10種類程度が確認されている。本図には5つのことわざが表現されているが、「上見れば方図なし」のような現在使われないものもある。

江戸後期 『浮世たとえ』 作者不詳
時田昌瑞ことわざコレクション 明治大学博物館所蔵

第二章

日本的國中學生熟知的常用成語諺語
200則（50音排序）

200 Best-known Idioms and Proverbs
for Junior High Graduates

101 開いた口が塞がらない 6級

日解與用法 ぽかんと**口を開けた**まま、何もしゃべれなくなった様子。相手の言葉や行動に、あきれ返って物が言えない状態をいう。

近義詞 茫然自失 4級

漢 張著嘴說不出話來。形容對對方逾越常理的發言或行為感到驚呆或厭惡時，一時愣得說不出話來，神情呆滯的樣子；

近 呆若木雞；張口結舌／瞠目結舌；啞然無聲；目瞪口呆

英 Temporarily **with one's mouth open**, be struck dumb with astonishment or disgust (at someone's words and actions).

近 (be) dumbfounded at (someone's behavior); (be) stunned into silence; (be) jaw-dropping

102 赤子の手を捻る 6級

日解與用法 **か弱い赤ちゃんの手を捻る。**弱い人を負かすことはたやすいことから、物事が簡単に行えることの喩え。

近義詞 朝飯前 5級　お茶の子さいさい 5級

漢 像**扭轉嬰兒的手掌**那樣小事一樁，比喻事情簡單非常容易完成。或比喻容易地打敗一個脆弱的對手。

近 易如反掌；輕而易舉；不費吹灰之力

英 Easy as **twisting an infant's arm**; Fig. Something exceptionally easy to do. Used when somebody requires little effort to finish something simple or defeat someone weaker.

近 (as) easy as pie; like taking candy from a baby; (as) easy as falling off a log; (like) child's play

103 揚げ足を取る 6級

日解與用法 相手が**蹴ろうとして揚げた足を取り**、逆に相手を倒す意。人の言い間違いや言葉じり、油断や無防備につけこんで、非難したり、からかったりすることをいう。

近義詞 ケチをつける 5級　小爪を拾う 4級

漢 **抓住對方抬起的腿**。比喻故意挑剔找差錯。對方不小心講錯話，說走了嘴，就找碴戲弄或攻擊。

近 挑語病；揪辮子；找碴、找岔子

英 **To grab another's raised leg** (while a wrestler make a move by raising his/her leg, he/she exposes his/her weakness at that moment); To find fault with what someone says or seize upon someone's mistake; To pounce on someone's slip of the tongue and take advantage of it.

近 cavil at someone's slip of the tongue; trip up (somebody on his/her wording)

104 足が棒になる 6級

日解與用法 長く立ったり、歩き続けたりして、**足の筋肉が棒のように**こわばって、疲れ果てた様子をいう。

近義詞 足が擂り粉木になる 3級

漢 站太久或走太多路，累得**兩腳僵直酸痛，像像棒子一樣**。比喻極度疲勞。

近 精疲力盡；兩腿發酸

英 Someone's **legs get as stiff as a board** (literally: bar or pole). A way to express that someone has very sore legs after taking a long walk or standing all the way.

近 walk one's legs off; worn out from walking; My feet are killing me. My dogs are barking.

105 明日は明日の風が吹く 6級

日解與用法 **明日が来れば明日の風が吹き**、状況も変わってくる。くよくよ先のことをを心配せず、成り行きに任せて生きるのがよいということ。物事はなるようになるのだという開き直りや、明日はまた新しい一日になるのだという慰めの言い回しとして使う。聖書にも似た表現がある。

近義詞 沈む瀬あれば浮かぶ瀬あり 3級

漢 **明天刮明天的風**。煩惱明天的事情白費心機，有問題明天再來面對。聖經裏亦有類似的詞句。

近 今朝有酒今朝醉，明日愁來明日當

英 **The winds of tomorrow will blow tomorrow.** As the saying in the Bible: "Take no thought for the morrow……" because tomorrow will care for itself. Things will turn out all right somehow.

近 Tomorrow is another day.; Tomorrow is a new day.; Sufficient unto the day is the evil thereof. (Bible); Everything will work out for the best.

106 当たって砕けろ 6級

日解與用法 **当たって砕けてしまえ**。成功するかどうか分からなくても、思いきってやってみよ。駄目元でやってみろ、一発勝負に出ることを言う。

近義詞 一か八か 6級 伸るか反るか 5級

漢 **竭盡全力撞擊衝破**。不管輸贏，不論成敗，姑且一試碰運氣。

近 孤注一擲；全力以赴

英 **To dash and smash it down**; To try one's luck. To take a chance; To give one's best shot.

近 Give it a shot. / Give it a try.; Go for broke.; Go hard or go home; put all eggs in one basket; put one's best foot forward

107 当たらずと雖も遠からず ⁶級

日解與用法 射た矢が**的に命中はしていなくとも、それほど外れてもいない**という こと。推測がぴったり当たっていなくても、それほどひどい間違いで ないことの喩え。中国礼記の原文の意味とニュアンスが違う。

近義詞 --

漢 雖未打中靶心，但離靶心並不遠。雖未 猜中，但相差不遠。與禮記原意相異。

近 八九不離十；（心誠求之）雖不中， 不遠矣《禮記・大學》

英 Fall short of the mark but a little wide of the mark. Fig. Good guess, not exactly correct but pretty close to the point (it carries differing views and ideas from the original Chinese saying).

近 Close, but no cigar.; You're not too far off.

108 痘痕も靨 ⁶級

日解與用法 相手に好意を持つと好意的な見方をし、**痘痕でさえ可愛らしい靨に見える** ということ。愛する者に対しては、欠点さえも長所に見えるという喩え。

近義詞 禿げが三年目につかぬ ³級 惚れた欲目 ³級 恋は思案の外 ³級 面々の 楊貴妃 ³級

漢 把戀人的瘡疤看成酒窩一樣可愛。比 喻愛情是盲目的，在情人眼裡對方無 一處不美。常言道：情人眼裡出西施 （「痘痕」指天花所留下的麻點瘡疤）。

近 情人眼裡出西施

英 When in love even pockmarks look like dimples; Fig. If you love someone, you can see no faults in that person. As the saying goes, "Beauty is in the eye of the beholder". Different people have different ideas about what is beautiful.

近 Love is blind.; Love sees no faults.; If Jack's in love, he's no judge of Jill's beauty.; think the sun shines out somebody's backside (vulgar)

109 危ない橋を渡る ⁶級

日解與用法 今にも落ちそうな**危険な橋を渡る**こと。目的を達成するために、危険 な手段をあえて使うことの喩え。特に法に触れ、すれすれのことをす る時に使う。

近義詞 剣の刃を渡る ³級 危ない綱渡りをする ³級

漢 過危險的橋。比喻膽大妄為，做有風 險的事。

近 鋌而走險

英 Endanger oneself by **crossing a broken bridge.** To do something that will make one open to danger; Usually referring to a person embarking on a hazardous attempt.

近 play with fire; walk a tightrope; stick one's neck out; go out on a limb; Necessity knows no law.; live on the edge

110 雨垂れ石を穿つ 6級

日解與用法 雨垂れでも長い間同じ所に落ち続ければ、ついには硬い石に穴を開ける。小さな力でも根気よく続けていれば、いつか成果が得られる、ということの喩え。中国の成語に由来。

近義詞 点滴石を穿つ 4級　石に立つ矢 3級

漢 水滴石穿，非一日之功。只要有恒心，不斷努力，事情一定成功。

近 水滴石穿（滴水穿石）；繩鋸木斷；鐵杵成針

英 **Dripping water penetrates the stone** (borrowed from a Chinese proverb); With enough time rain drops eat away stones. Something you say to encourage someone to be persistent. You can achieve your aim as long as you try hard without giving up. Indomitable perseverance effort can overcome any difficulties.

近 Constant dropping wears away a stone.; Little strokes fell great oaks.

111 言うは易く行うは難し 6級

日解與用法 言うだけなら簡単で誰にでもできるが、それを実行するのは難しい。

近義詞 口では大阪の城も建つ 3級

漢 說來容易做來難。比喻說明事情的道理較易，實行其事則較難。

近 言之易而行之難；看花容易，繡花難

英 **Easy to say, hard to do.** Easier said than done. There is a great difference between word and deed, because saying is one thing and doing is another.

近 Easier said than done.; Who will bell the cat? (Aesop)

112 医者の不養生* 6級

日解與用法 人に養生を勧める医者が、自分の健康に注意を払わないこと。また、立派な理屈を言いながら、実行が伴わないこと。

近義詞 坊主の不信心 4級　学者の不身持ち 4級　易者身の上知らず 1級　陰陽師身の上知らず* 4級

漢 醫生規勸別人留意健康，說得頭頭是道，自己反而忽略養生之道。說的是一套，做的又是另外一套。好似有人忙著解決別人的問題，卻處理不了自己的難題。

近 能醫不自醫；言行不一；知而不行

英 **A doctor who is careless of one's own health.** Said about a doctor who is busy curing the diseases of others but often neglects his/her own well-being. When a physician disregards his/her own health like that, he/she failed to practice what he/she preached or he/she was all talk with nothing to back it up.

近 Physician, heal thyself.; Practice what you preach.; (be) All talk and no action.; talk the talk, but don't walk the walk

113 板に付く 6級

日解與用法 役者の演技が上達し、**板張りの舞台にしっくりと調和していることを**いう。また、仕事に慣れてぎこちなさがなくなり、物腰や服装もその仕事に相応しく見えて違和感のないさまををいう。

近義詞 様になる 6級　堂に入る 3級

漢 演員的演技逐漸地純熟，與舞台的氣氛很相稱。形容一個人適應工作後，態度、神色很自然，舉止、造型也恰如其分，與其職業搭配的很和諧。

近 爐火純青；得心應手

英 **To get used to stage career** and to become an expert. Fig. A compliment to describe someone's manner or outfit which looks good enough to be shown publicly after adapting oneself to a new position or career, brought to the peak of perfection.

近 make a good fist of (doing something); (be perfectly) at home in (something); (be) in one's element

114 一か八か 6級

日解與用法 サイコロを振って、丁（偶数）か半（奇数）かをあてて勝負を決める博打から出た表現だといわれている。**一は「丁」の、八は「半」の漢字の上の部分を取って隠語として用いた。**出たとこ勝負でやってみる、または、運を天に任せてやってみる時に言う言葉。

近義詞 丁か半か 4級　伸るか反るか 4級

漢 不是一就是八（源自擲骰子賭博的隱語。「一」「八」各取自「丁」「半」上半部。丁為偶數的骰子點，半為奇數的骰子點）。不管好歹孤注一擲，不是全勝就是大敗。一切聽天由命了。

近 一擲乾坤

英 **Either one or eight** of the dice in games (a kind of buzzword for gambling), means either an ace or a loss, like playing a high-stakes game. Fig. To solve a problem either fail completely or be very successful; To give something a try, no matter how bad things get.

近 kill or cure; sink or swim; make or break; win or lose

115 一期一会 6級

日解與用法 一生に**一度だけの巡り合わせ。**二度と巡っては来ない、この大切なご縁を思い残すことのないように、今出来る最高のおもてなしをしよう、と言う千利休の茶道の心得である。

近義詞 一世一代 3級

漢 一生中僅此一次的相遇。向來不認識的人偶然相遇，即使只是一面之交也要珍惜此因緣際會。日本安土桃山時代著名的茶道宗師千利休的茶道心得。

英 **One lifetime, one meeting.** An idea of *Sen no Rikyū*, the founder of the "Way of Tea" in Japan. He reminds us that each moment, each meeting will happen only once. If you meet any person as if it were the last time, you might as well extend a warm hospitality and cherish each once-in-a-lifetime acquaintance.

近 cherish a serendipitous encounter

近 萍水相逢

116 一難去ってまた一難 6級

日解與用法 一つの災難を切り抜けてやれやれと思う間もなく、**別の災難が降りかかる**。次々に災難が襲ってくることや、人生は試練に満ちていることの喩え。

近義詞 前門の虎後門の狼 6級　　虎口を逃れて竜穴に入る 4級

漢　避開一個災難，而另外的災難又乘隙而入。逃過一個難關又進了一個難關，狀況越來越糟。亦比喻人生充滿考驗。

近　一波未平，一波又起；前門拒虎，後門進狼

英　**One misfortune goes, another comes.** When you get out of one problem, but find yourself in an even worse situation. A new problem arises before the old one is solved. Life is filled with ordeal.

近　(jump) out of the frying pan into the fire

117 一年の計は元旦にあり 6級

日解與用法 一年の計画は年の初めである元旦に立てるべきである。物事を始めるにあたっては、最初にきちんとした計画を立てるのが肝要だという意味。

近義詞 一日の計は朝にあり 6級

漢　新年是一年的開始，萬象更新，就應該要有新的規劃，為全年的工作設定好基礎乃為成功的要訣。比喻凡事起頭時須好好計畫未來。

近　一年之計在於春，一日之計在於晨

英　**The whole year's plans are made on New Year's Day.** An expression indicating that an earlier planning is the key to success. The whole year's work depends on a good start for the New Year. Fig. Making a New Year resolution is important and meaningful.

近　Plan your year in the spring, your day at dawn.; A good beginning makes a good ending.

118 一目置く 6級

日解與用法 囲碁から生まれた言葉。弱い方が先に**一目の石を置いて**対局を始めることをいう。能力が自分より優れた人に対して、その実力を認め敬意を払うこと。

近義詞 頭が下がる 6級

漢　下圍棋時，較弱的一方先下一步（先走一格），示意自己略遜一籌並向對方的本事表達欽佩之意。

近　另眼看待

英　In Japanese *IGO*, a weaker player is **allowed to place their piece first** as a handicap, a way to acknowledge someone's superiority and treat him or her with due respect.

近　take off one's hat to (a person); take a back seat

119 一文惜しみの百知らず 6級
いちもん お ひゃく し

日解與用法 一文ほどの僅かな**金にこだわり**、全体としての利益に考えが及ばず、
いちもん わず かね
後で**百文の大損を招く**。目先の損得しか頭に浮かばず、見通しが利か
あと ひゃくもん おおぞん まね めさき そんとく あたま う みとお き
ないということの喩え。
たと

近義詞 一文惜しみの百損 4級　小利をむさぼって大利を失う 3級
いちもん お ひゃくぞん しょうり だいり うしな

漢 省一文錢損失百文錢。小筆錢精明，大
筆錢浪費。意指佔小便宜反而吃大虧。

近 因小失大；殺雞取卵；惜指失掌；揀
了芝麻，丟了西瓜

英 **Thrifty with one *mon* (small coin) yet not careful
enough about spending hundreds.** Describes someone who suffers a big loss for a little gain or overlooks
large expenses to save a little money.

近 Penny wise and pound foolish.; Spoil the ship for a halfpen-
ny's worth of tar.; Kill the goose that lays the golden egg(s).

120 一を聞いて十を知る* 6級
いち き じゅう し

日解與用法 物事の**一端を聞いた**だけで、**その全体像を理解する**。非常に聡明で理
ものごと いったん き ぜんたいぞう りかい ひじょう そうめい り
解が早く、洞察力が鋭いことの喩え。中国の成語に由来。
かい はや どうさつりょく するど たと ちゅうごく せいご ゆらい

近義詞 告往知来 4級　目から鼻へ抜ける 4級
こくおうちらい め はな ぬ

漢 一個聰明善解又有洞察力的人，只要
聽到一點苗頭就能立即理解全貌。

近 聞一知十；舉一反三；觸類旁通

英 **Drop a hint, and understand ten other things.**
(borrowed from a Chinese proverb) Fig. A brief ex-
planation is enough for a person who is quick on the
uptake. You only have to hint at something to wise
people in order to get them to understand it.

近 (A) word to the wise is enough/sufficient.; (A) nod is
as good as a wink.; Send a wise man on an errand, and
say nothing unto him.

121 一寸先は闇* 6級
いっすんさき やみ

日解與用法 闇夜ではほんの**少し先でも真っ暗で**何も見えないように、ごく近い将
やみよ すこ さき ま くら なに み ちか しょう
来のことでも全く見えない。どんな運命が待ち受けているのか予測が
らい まった み うんめい ま う よそく
つかないということの喩え。「一寸」は約 3.03cm、僅かな距離を指す。
たと いっすん やく センチ わず きょり さ
仏教の無常観から生まれたことわざ。
ぶっきょう むじょうかん う

近義詞 無常の風は時を選ばず 3級
むじょう かぜ とき えら

漢 近在咫尺的前方是一片漆黑，什麼都
看不見。比喻不久的將來會發生甚麼
事情誰也無法預測。人生無常，世事
難料。出自佛教無常觀的說法。

近 前途未卜／前途莫測；今日不知明日
事，上床難保下床時；天有不測風雲

英 **It's all darkness even one *sun* (*sun*≒1.2 inches) ahead.**
It means that you don't even know what the future will
bring, even in a few seconds. No one knows what the
future holds, because life is unpredictable and uncertain.
It's one of teachings of the Buddha about impermanence.

近 The unexpected always happens.; You never know
what life has in store for you.; You never know what's
around the corner.

122 一石二鳥 6級

いっせき に ちょう

日解與用法 **一つの石**を投げて、**二羽の鳥**を打ち落とす。一つの行為で、同時に二つの利益・効果を上げることの喩え。英語圏のことわざの語訳。

近義詞 一挙両得 5級
いっきょりょうとく

漢 只丢了**一個石頭**卻同時抓到**兩隻鳥**。比喻做一件事，同時達到兩個目的或得到兩種好處。源自英文的諺語。

近 一箭雙鵰；一舉兩得

英 Killing **two birds** with **one stone**. To solve two problems at one time with a single action or to accomplish two tasks with only one effort. (taken from an English proverb)

近 Kill two birds with one stone.

123 居ても立ってもいられない 6級

い た

日解與用法 気持ちが高ぶって、**座っても立っても**いられない。心配したり興奮したりして、落ち着かなくて、じっとしていられない様子を言う。

近義詞 矢も楯もたまらず 4級
や たて

漢 坐著也不是，站著也不是。形容情緒不安，心神不寧，焦急煩躁的樣子。

近 坐立不安；侷促不安；坐臥不寧；如坐針氈

英 **Feel uneasy whether sitting or standing.** Cannot sit still; To be on tenterhooks with anxiety or unable to contain oneself for joy.

近 have ants in one's pants; sit on pins and needles; like a cat on a hot tin roof

124 鰯の頭も信心から * 6級

いわし あたま しんじん

日解與用法 つまらない**鰯の頭**であっても、**信心して**神棚に祀っていれば、有難い尊い存在になるということの喩え。つまらないものを信じ込んでいる人を揶揄する言葉としても使われる。昔の日本では鬼除けのため、節分（立春前日）の夜に鰯の頭を柊の枝に刺して玄関先に飾る習慣があった。

近義詞 竹箒も五百羅漢 3級 白紙も信心次第 3級
たけぼうき ごひゃくらかん しらかみ しんじんしだい

漢 信者為真。即使不顯眼的沙丁魚頭，只要信仰它也會靈驗。也可用來揶揄人冥頑不靈的態度或嘲諷人迷信過度。古時家家戶戶會在節分（立春前日）這天夜晚將插有沙丁魚頭的柊樹枝葉放置於門口，用以驅邪。

近 心誠則靈；精誠所至，金石為開

英 **Even the head of a sardine can be deified in a faith.** Fig. Faith can be based on anything you firmly believed or appreciated as long as you are pious. Sometimes used as a phrase to tease about someone's mistaken belief. In olden days, the head of sardines with holly leaves were used as a ceremonial decoration at the front door to drive off evil spirits, especially on the day before *Setsubun* (beginning of spring of the lunar calendar).

近 Faith will move mountains.; Miracles happen to those who believe in them.

125 上には上がある 6級

日解與用法 レベルが**最も上だと思っても、世の中には、さらにその上の優れたものがある**ということの喩え。素晴らしいものを見て感嘆したり呆れたりする時の気持ちを表す言葉として使う。

近義詞 上を見れば方図がない 3級

漢 指才能再高，在這世上還有比自己更有才華的人，勸戒人不要夜郎自大。也可用於欽佩或諷刺的場面。

近 人外有人，天外有天；強中自有強中手；一山還有一山高

英 **No matter how clever you are, there's always someone outwits you.** Fig. There's always somebody a notch better than you. Sometimes this term is used with an admirable or ironic intent, or reminding people that there is always something more to learn.

近 Diamond cuts diamond.

126 雨後の筍 6級

日解與用法 雨が降った後の春の竹林には、**筍**が続々と生えてくる。同じような物事が相次いで現れることの喩え。

近義詞 間を置かずに

漢 春天下雨後竹筍一下子就長出來很多。比喻新生事物迅速大量地湧現出來。

近 雨後春筍

英 **Like bamboo shoots right after the spring rain.** A metaphor of a rapid and/or sudden new growth, or many new things emerge in rapid succession.

近 spring up like mushrooms

127 氏より育ち* 6級

日解與用法 人は**家柄や身分よりも、育てられ方が大切**である。育つ環境や教育が人間の形成に強い影響を与えるということの喩え。

近義詞 家柄より芋茎 3級　性相近し、習い相遠し 2級

漢 教養重於家世。比喻門第高莫如教養好，後天的教育及環境對人格的形成影響非常大，大於先天因素，大於家業身世。

近 養育重於生育

英 **Upbringing rather than parentage.** Education rather than family lineage. It implies that birth is much, but breeding is more. Personality is very much affected by the education acquired after birth, not determined by bloodline alone.

近 Nurture is above nature.

128 嘘つきは泥棒の始まり* 6級

日解與用法 平気で**嘘を言う**ようになれば、良心の呵責を感じなくなって**盗みも**平気に**始める**ようになるから、嘘はついてはいけないという戒め。

近義詞 嘘と盗みは隣り合わせ 4級　嘘は盗みのもと 4級

漢 撒謊是偷竊的開端。覺得說謊無所謂而不感到羞恥，日久之後習慣成自然，變本加厲開始行竊。警告人們不要撒謊，「勿以惡小而為之」。

近 小時偷針，大時偷金；謊近盜，騙近賊

英 **A liar is the groundwork for a thief.** One who will lie, will steal. A petty dishonesty (lying) will eventually become a big crookery so don't even start.

近 He that will steal an egg will steal an ox.; Lying and stealing are next door neighbors.; Show me a liar, and I'll show thee a thief.

129 売り言葉に買い言葉* 6級

日解與用法 **相手の乱暴な言葉に対して、同じような調子で言い返す**こと。「売り言葉」とは、ものを売りつける時に言う言葉。転じて、相手にわざと喧嘩を仕掛ける (売る) ような言葉のこと。

近義詞 問い声よければ応え声よい 3級

漢 你一言我一語，有人用粗言故意挑釁，對方就不甘示弱以穢語回嘴。比喻雙方以刻薄尖銳的言詞相互奚落。抬槓，鬥嘴，唱反調。

近 針鋒相對；尖言冷語；一報還一報；以眼還眼，以牙還牙；唇槍舌劍；一句來，一句去

英 **Buying** (inflammatory) **words for selling** (quarreling) **words.** Fig. To pick fighting words by using equally harsh words, retort an argument against, exchange of insults (in an angry fashion).

近 give as good as one gets; serve someone the same sauce; return like for like; pay someone back in their own coin; give someone a taste of their own medicine

130 瓜の蔓に茄子はならぬ* 6級

日解與用法 **瓜の蔓には瓜しか実らず、茄子はならない。** 平凡な親から非凡な子は生まれない、血統は争えないということの喩え。また、ある原因からはそれ相応の結果しか生じないということの喩え。

近義詞 燕雀鳳を生まず 3級　鳩の卵が鴨にはならぬ 3級

漢 瓜秧不長茄子。比喻子女的才能或資質像父母，平凡的父母生不了優秀的子女。也比喻有其因必有其果。

近 烏鴉生不出鳳凰；有其因必有其果

英 **A gourd vine does not bear an eggplant.** A metaphor to express that ordinary parents will not produce wonder children, because people tend to raise children who are like themselves.

近 Like breeds like.; Eagles do not breed doves.; An onion will not produce a rose.; A bad tree does not yield good apples.; Of evil grain no good seed can come.

131 瓜二つ ⑥級

日解與用法 瓜を縦二つに割ると、切り口の左右の形はそっくり。親子・兄弟などの顔かたちが、見分けがつかないほどよく似ていることの喩え。

近義詞 そっくりさん

漢 好像切成兩片的瓜一樣，非常相似，分不出哪一邊是哪一邊。比喻相貌外表酷似，如同一個模子刻出來的。

近 長得一模一樣

英 **Two lengthwise halves of a squash or melon.** Said that two persons with perfectly identical faces or appearance, used when someone is a perfect lookalike of his/her parents or someone else.

近 (be) like two peas in a pod; (be) the spitting image of ～ ; (be) cast in the same mold; (be a) chip off the old block; (be) cut from the same cloth

132 噂をすれば影がさす ⑥級

日解與用法 その場にいない**人の噂をしていると、たまたま噂の本人が**ひょっこり**現れる**ことがある。「影がさす」は、姿が見えるの意味。人の噂や悪口はほどほどにするべきだという戒め。

近義詞 人事言わば筵敷け ③級

漢 正在閒聊到某人的事即看到某人的影子出現。比喻談論到某人，某人湊巧就來了。隱喻不要在人背後說壞話。

近 說曹操，曹操就到

英 **Talk about a certain person, and that person appears** unexpectedly. Used when you are talking about someone and they show up. Could be used as a notion that don't go overboard on gossiping behind someone's back.

近 Speak of the devil (and he shall appear).

133 縁の下の力持ち* ⑥級

日解與用法 **建物の荷重を見えない縁側の下で支える丈夫な柱**のように、人知れずに、陰で他人のために苦労や努力をすること。また、そのような人の喩え。人のために役に立っているのに報われないといった意味合いでも使う。

近義詞 縁の下の掃除番 ③級　縁の下の舞 ③級

漢 像陽台走廊下面支撐著的支柱一樣，看不見。意指為別人默默耕耘，賣力工作或指這種任勞任怨但鮮為人知的人。也指空為別人辛苦而得不到回報的人。

近 為人作嫁；吃力不討好；無名英雄；幕後功臣

英 **Like bracing struts of veranda**, inconspicuous but reliable. Fig.Someone who is willing to undertake a thankless job but never expects any credit or gets no praise for doing it. Unsung hero.

近 (works hard from) behind the scenes; thankless job

134 岡目八目／傍目八目 _{6級}

岡目八目／傍目八目（おかめはちもく／おかめはちもく）

日解與用法 囲碁を**傍から見ている者は、**対局者より**八目先まで見通せる**という意。当事者よりも傍観者の方が、冷静で客観的に物事が見える。

近義詞 脇目にはよく見える _{4級}　他人の正目 _{3級}

漢 看別人下將棋可以看得比較清楚大局，可預想到往後的八步棋。比喻處理事情時，若非身處其中的當事者，往往會比較冷靜客觀。

近 當局者迷，旁觀者清

英 **Onlooker** (while watching Japanese *IGO*) **can see eight moves ahead**; Fig. People who see things from the vantage point are better able to see the "bigger picture" of what is actually happening. Outsiders usually get a clearer grasp of the situation.

近 Lookers-on see most of the game.; Men are blind in their own cause.

135 驕る平家は久しからず _{6級}

驕る平家は久しからず（おごるへいけはひさしからず）

日解與用法 栄華を極めた**平家の天下も傲慢な振る舞い**のため、長くは続かなかったことから、地位や財力を鼻にかけ、驕り高ぶる者は遠からず落ちぶれることを喩える。勢いが盛んな時ほど慎まねばならないという戒め。

近義詞 驕れる者久しからず _{4級}　物盛んなれば則ち衰う _{4級}　喜んで尻餅をつく _{4級}

漢 平氏一族因高傲自大其興盛未能持久。意指有錢有勢的人若趾高氣揚、目中無人，總有遭到挫敗的一天。暗示人成功時不能太驕傲。

近 驕者必敗；滿招損，謙受益

英 **If the *Taira* clan would have humility, it would last long.** Used as a warning not to act arrogant and conceited. Haughty demeanor and ostentatious display will be doomed to failure, and fall victim to its own arrogance.

近 Pride will have a fall.; Pride goes before destruction.

136 お茶を濁す _{6級}

お茶を濁す（ちゃをにごす）

日解與用法 茶道の作法をよく知らない者が、いい加減なやり方でお茶をたて、**濁らせてそれらしいお茶に見えるように**し、その場を取り繕うこと。適当なことを言ったりしたりして、一時しのぎにその場をごまかすことの喩え。

近義詞 言葉を濁す _{5級}

漢 不懂茶道的人隨便泡茶攪濁茶水敷衍了事。比喻含糊其詞，為了搪塞某事，以似是而非的說辭牽強應付。

近 支吾以對；打馬虎眼；顧左右而言他

英 A person who is unfamiliar with tea making **rushes through a tea ceremony by roiling the tea.** To get out of an uncomfortable situation by cooking up a specious excuse or giving someone the runaround or avoiding the subject with an evasive answer.

近 take the easy way out; hem and haw

137 同じ穴の狢* 6級

日解與用法 同じ穴で生活する狢。一見したところでは悪い連中の仲間に見えないが、実際は同じくたちの悪い者であることの喩え。通常、よくないことをする人に言う。

近義詞 同じ穴の狸 5級　一つ穴の狐 5級

漢 同棲在一個土山裡的狢。比喻乍看之下形同陌路，實際上彼此是勾結在一起作壞事的搭擋。

近 一丘之貉；狐群狗黨；臭味相投

英 **Badgers from the same lair.** Usually refers to the villains of the same stripe, they are all just as bad as each other.

近 two of a kind; (as) thick as thieves; (be) hand and glove with each other

138 思い立ったが吉日* 6級

日解與用法 何かをしようと思ったら、その日を縁起の良い日としてすぐに取りかかるのが良いということ。事を始めようと決意したら、ただちに着手すべし、今日成し得ることは明日に延ばすな、という教え。

近義詞 善は急げ* 6級　好機逸すべからず 4級　旨い物は宵に食え 3級

漢 心動不如馬上行動，想辦某些事的那天就是黃道吉日。提醒人時機難得，必需抓緊。想做什麼事就應該即刻付諸行動。今天能做的事不要拖到明天。

近 日日是好日；機不可失，時不再來；擇日不如撞日

英 **The day in which you decide to do it, is your lucky day.** It reminds people that "Never put off till tomorrow what you can do today". Carpe diem, means "seize the day".

近 There is no time like the present.; Opportunity knocks but once.; The mill cannot grind with water that is past.; Tomorrow never comes.

139 親の心子知らず* 6級

日解與用法 子を思う親の深い愛情を知らずに、子供は好き勝手に振る舞うということ。自分が親になってみなければ親心は理解できないという心境を表す言葉、また、子供を叱る時の小言にも使う。

近義詞 子を持って知る親の恩 5級

漢 父母含辛茹苦養育兒女，而**子女卻不知父母愛護自己的心意**。子女往往任性放縱，處處與父母作對。此句用於感嘆自己做父母才體會出當年父母養育子女的艱辛。有時也用於嘮叨兒女不聽管教時。

近 （當家才知鹽米貴）養兒方知父母恩

英 **Children never know what is on their parents' mind.** Something that you say in order to remind yourself or advice your kids that "People won't know how indebted they are to their parents till they become parents". There is no love like that of parents'.

近 We never know the love of a parent till we become parents ourselves. (Henry Ward Beecher 格言)

140 親の脛をかじる 6級

日解與用法 **親の脛をかじるとは、親の労働に頼る**意。成人しても結婚しても自立できず、親に養われ、親の経済的援助で生活することの喩え。脛は膝からくるぶしまでの部位をいう。人が立って働くのを支える大事な部分で、一所懸命に働くことを指している。

近義詞 親がかり

漢 咬住父母的小腿，意指依靠父母的幹活。形容長大或成家後的子女經濟上無法獨立，仍舊受父母贍養或仰賴父母的接濟度日。

近 扶不起的阿斗；啃老族；揩父母的油

英 **To chew on the shank of one's parents.** A saying referring to a young adult who is dependent, banking on one's parents' help.

近 sponge off one's parents

141 親の七光り 6級

日解與用法 親の地位や名声が高いと、大きい光となって子を照らす。**親の威光によって子が恩恵を受けること**。また、親の力を子が大いに利用して出世することの喩え。（「七」は、数が多いことを表す）

近義詞 親の光は七光り 6級

漢 得父母七道光芒的庇蔭。比喻攀援有錢有勢的父母親往上爬，利用父母的社會背景出人頭地。

近 沾老子光

英 **Parents' sevenfold luster.** A metaphor that refers to the way to move up the career ladder by capitalizing on parents' fame or the way to owe success to parents' authority.

近 ride on parents' coattails

142 終わりよければ全て良し 6級

日解與用法 終わりが大事。**締めくくりが良ければすべて評価される**ということ。物事は結末さえ素晴らしければ、発端や過程は問題にならないということの喩え。シェイクスピアの戯曲「All's well that ends well」の訳語。

近義詞 有終の美を飾る 4級　掉尾を飾る 4級

漢 結果好就一切都好。意指善終為善皆大歡喜，即使起頭或過程並不盡理想。源自莎士比亞的喜劇標題「終成眷屬 All's well that ends well」。

近 有終之美

英 **An event that has a good ending is good** even if some things went wrong in the beginning or along the way (a direct translation of the expression from the title of a play by Shakespeare).

近 All's well that ends well.; The end crowns all.

143 女心と秋の空 6級

日解與用法 変わりやすい**秋の空模様**のように、**女性の心が移ろい**やすいということ。人に対する愛情に限らず、感情の起伏が激しいことや移り気なことをも指す。

近義詞 女の心は猫の目 4級

漢 女人的心與秋天的天氣。比喻女人的心思像秋天的天氣一樣變化多端，忽晴忽雨，捉摸不透。

近 女人的心，秋天的雲；女人心，海底針；水性楊花

英 **Woman's heart and autumn skies.** A metaphor that refers to woman's feelings are hard to read, as fickle as autumn weather, as changeable as a weathercock.

近 (A) woman's mind and winter wind change oft.

144 おんぶに抱っこ 6級

日解與用法 子供を**負ぶってやると、子供は次に抱っこをしてと**甘えてくるさまから、何から何まで他人に甘え、世話になることを喩える。一人では何も出来ないといった意を含み、大抵は非難の言葉として使われる。

近義詞 負ぶえば抱かりょう 4級

漢 像小嬰兒一樣，這次背著，下次叫著要抱。意指一個凡事依賴別人，得到一些幫助後，進而還想得到更多幫助。通常含譴責之意。

近 得寸進尺；得了屋子想上炕

英 **Hug in one's arms right after piggyback ride**; If you carry baby on your back and it wants to be held in your arms soon. Fig. Something that you describe or blame a person who is wholly relying on you, or will demand more when you're generous to him/her.

近 Give someone an inch and he'll take a mile/yard.; Give a clown your finger and he will take your hand.

145 恩を仇で返す* 6級

日解與用法 **恩を施してくれた人に対して、感謝して恩返しするどころか害を加え**るような**仕打ちをする**行為を指す。

近義詞 飼い犬に手を嚙まれる* 6級　後足で砂をかける 4級　庇を貸して母屋を取られる 4級

漢 拿怨恨回報所受的恩惠。指忘恩負義。

近 恩將仇報；以怨報德；吃裡扒外；過河拆橋；吃曹操的米，講劉備的話；卸磨殺驢

英 **Repay kindness with hostility** or ingratitude, it means to treat someone badly who has helped you in some way or to hurt someone who does good things for you.

近 return evil for good; kick away/down the ladder; bite the hand that feeds you; The beggar pays a benefit with a louse.; The axe goes to the wood from whence it borrowed its helve.

146 顔から火が出る 6級

日解與用法 きまり悪くて、恥ずかしさのあまり、**顔が火照って真っ赤になる**様子を言う。赤面の度合いは「耳の付け根まで真っ赤になる」という表現に近い。

近義詞 穴があったら入りたい 6級　顔に紅葉を散らす 4級

漢 因尷尬羞愧而滿臉通紅，好像臉上快噴出火一樣。其羞愧的程度接近「臉紅紅到耳根」的意思。

近 面紅耳赤；羞愧難當

英 **Fire comes from a face** with shame. When someone is deeply ashamed of oneself, his or her face is red with embarrassment.

近 blush with shame; go beetroot/go as red as a beetroot

147 顔に泥を塗る 6級

日解與用法 **相手の顔に汚い泥を塗り**、名誉を傷つけて面目を失わせる、また、恥をかかせることの喩え。

近義詞 顔を汚す 5級　顔を潰す 5級

漢 在他人臉孔塗泥巴。比喻使某人名譽掃地，顏面盡失，出醜蒙羞。

近 讓人顏面無光；丟人現眼

英 **To fling mud or get dirt on a person's face**, a way to say when someone disgraces a family/friend's name or makes them lose their faces; To bring shame upon another.

近 drag someone's name through the mire

148 火中の栗を拾う 6級

日解與用法 自分の利益にはならないのに、そそのかされて他人のために危険を冒すこと。また、困難な問題に身を乗り出すことの喩え。猿におだてられた**猫が囲炉裏で焼けている栗を拾った**が、栗は猿に食べられてしまい、猫は火傷をした、という 17 世紀のフランスの寓話ラ・フォンテーヌから。

近義詞 --

漢 取爐火裡烤熟的栗子。比喻被慫恿去為別人冒風險，自己卻一無所得。或比喻自願被捲入問題卻得不到好處。故事見 17 世紀法國詩人拉・封登的寓言。

近 火中取栗

英 Succeed in a hazardous or unpleasant undertaking for someone else's benefit, with reference to the French fable of La Fontaine of the 17th century, about a monkey **using a cat's paw to extract roasting chestnuts from a fire.**

近 pull someone's chestnuts out of the fire

149 河童の川流れ 6級

日解與用法 泳ぎのうまい**河童**でも、**川の流れに押し流されてしまう**ことがある。どんな名人でも、時には失敗をすることの喩え。また、自信があり過ぎ、調子に乗って油断していると失敗する、という戒め。

近義詞 弘法にも筆の誤り* 6級　猿も木から落ちる* 6級　上手の手から水が漏る 5級　千慮の一失 4級

漢 河童也會被河水沖走。指對某些事很熟練的人反而疏忽導致失敗。也提醒人不要太自以為有本領。(註：河童為日本傳說中之棲水邊的生物，諳水性)

近 善游者溺，善騎者墮；百密必有一疏；智者千慮，必有一失

英 Even a good swimmer like **a *kappa* sometimes drowns when going against the flow of river**. A way to remind people that don't get too confident (*kappa* is an imaginary water sprite found in Japanese folklore, was believed that it was good at swimming).

近 Even the best hack stumbles once.; A good marksman may miss.

150 我田引水 6級

日解與用法 **自分の田んぼにだけ水を引き入れる**ことから、他人のことを考えずに、自分に都合が良いように考え、自分の利益になるように計らい、自分の思い通りに振る舞うさまを表す。

近義詞 手前勝手 4級

漢 往自家田裏灌水。比喻把好處全部留給自己，自私自利。

近 肥水不落外人田

英 Strain to **draw water for one's own paddy**. Fig. A self-centered person who is full of himself/herself and seeking his/her own profits.

近 Every miller draws water to his own mill.; Keep your ain fish-guts to your ain sea-maws.

151 壁に耳あり障子に目あり* 6級

日解與用法 どこかで誰かが**壁に耳をあてて聞いている**かも知れない。**障子に穴をあけて覗き見している**かも知れない。隠し事や密談は漏れやすいことの喩え。人と話をする時は第三者に聞かれないように用心せよという戒め。

近義詞 壁に耳あり徳利に口あり 4級　昼には目あり夜には耳あり 4級

漢 隔著一道牆也有人偷聽，隔著一扇紙門也有人偷看。比喻即使秘密協商的事或個人的隱私總會走漏風聲。也用於勸人說話小心，任何事難以掩人耳目。

近 隔牆有耳；牆有縫，壁有耳；路上說話，草裡有人

英 **Walls have ears, paper sliding doors have eyes.** A warning that one should be careful about saying something as someone may overhear the conversation.

近 Walls have ears.; Fields have eyes, and woods have ears.

152 聞くは一時の恥、聞かぬは一生の恥* 6級

日解與用法 知らないことを人に聞くのは、その時は恥ずかしいと思っても、聞かなければ一生知らぬまま過ごすことになり、もっと恥ずかしい。知らないことは積極的に質問するべきだという教え。

近義詞 問うは一旦の恥、問わぬは末代の恥 4級　下問を恥じず 4級

漢 問乃一時之恥，不問乃終身之羞。意指不知則問，向人求教不過一時蒙羞，不問的人則永遠愚昧，一生羞愧。訓勉人鼓起勇氣請教他人可以受益無窮。

近 不恥下問；不懂裝懂，永世飯桶

英 **Asking makes one appear foolish for a moment, but one who does not ask makes one foolish for one's entire life.** The saying tells us not to claim to know something that we don't know but rather we get wise by asking questions. If we pretend to understand when we don't, we'll remain in ignorance. In other words, we'd better swallow our pride and ask for advice.

近 Better to ask the way than go astray.; A man becomes learned by asking questions.

---

153 疑心暗鬼を生ず 6級

日解與用法 疑いの心を持つと、いるはずのない鬼の姿が暗闇の中に見えたりする。猜疑心があると、何でもないことまで怪しく思えてしまい、何でもないことでも恐ろしく感じてしまうことの喩え。中国の成語に由来。

近義詞 杯中の蛇影 4級　落ち武者は薄の穂にも怖ず 3級

漢 疑懼產生暗中看到鬼的幻覺。過度猜忌和懷疑作祟，就容易無中生有，自己嚇自己。

近 疑心生暗鬼；疑神疑鬼；杯弓蛇影；草木皆兵

英 **Mistrust calls forth ogres** (borrowed from a Chinese proverb). Fig. Mistrust and suspicion often gives a small thing a big shadow, it generates fear in the mind, too. Thus, keep the mind clear of doubts, otherwise you will even be afraid of your own shadow.

近 Worry often gives a small thing a big shadow.

---

154 九死に一生を得る 6級

日解與用法 何度(九度)も死ぬような危険な状況になりながら、何とか生き延びるという意味から、助かる見込みがほぼ無いところで奇跡的に命拾いしたことを指す。「九死」とは、九分通り助からないという際どい状態と解釈することもできる。

近義詞 危機一髪で助かる 5級

漢 歷經多次(九次)近於生死關頭的險境猶能存活。比喻倖免於難。「九死」也可解釋為「死的機率有九成、活的希望只有一成」，極其危急的狀況。

近 九死一生；死裡逃生；千鈞一髮

英 **To secure one life from nine deaths**; Fig. To have a near/narrow escape from the jaws of death. Survival after many hazards. A near go (British).

近 have a close call/shave

155 窮鼠猫を嚙む ^{6級}

日解與用法 追い詰められて**逃げ場を失った鼠は、猫に嚙みつく**。絶体絶命の窮地になれば、弱者でも死に物狂いで強敵に立ち向かうということの喩え。

近義詞 窮寇は追うことなかれ ^{2級}

漢 無路可逃的老鼠被逼急，也會反過來咬貓。比喻受人欺壓到了走投無路時，不顧後果，明知敵不過也會拼死反抗。

近 窮鼠齧貓；窮寇莫追

英 **A cornered rat bites the cat**; Fig. A person at bay will take daring action right away, when left with no option even someone weak or desperate will fight, they will turn bad fortune into chance.

近 A baited cat may grow as fierce as a lion.; Despair gives courage to a coward.; Put a coward to his mettle and he'll fight the devil.

156 漁夫の利 ^{6級}

日解與用法 鷸とハマグリが争っている間に、**漁師が**両方とも捕らえた、という中国「戦国策」の故事に由来する表現。当事者同士が争っている隙に、関係のない第三者が何の苦労もなく**利益を横取りする**ことの喩え。

近義詞 鷸蚌の争い ^{4級}　犬兎の争い ^{4級}

漢 鷸去啄蚌，嘴被蚌殻夾住，兩方面都不相讓。結果漁翁來了把兩個都捉住。比喻利用別人的爭執矛盾而從中獲利。

近 鷸蚌相爭，漁翁得利；坐收漁利；坐享其成

英 **A fisherman's profit** (borrowed from a Chinese saying). When the sandpiper and the clam grapple, the fisherman benefits from the conflict and catches both. Fig. To reap the spoils of war without lifting a finger, to reap a third-party profit.

近 While two dogs are fighting for a bone, a third runs away with it.; Whilst the dogs are growling at each other the wolf devours the sheep.; play both ends against the middle; fish in troubled waters

157 口八丁手八丁 ^{6級}

日解與用法 手八丁といわれる人は櫓が八つある小舟を自由自在に操る達人であるという説がある。「丁」は細長い物を数えるのに用い、八丁は「巧み」という意で使われる。**話すことも達者で、手を使って何かをすることも器用である**ことをいう。軽々しいという皮肉なニュアンスを込めて用いることが多い。

近義詞 口も八丁手も八丁 ^{6級}

漢 一個口靈手巧、能說又能幹的人，像是有八張嘴巴和能一次划有八支槳的小船的人。可用於形容人口齒伶俐精明能幹，也常用於挖苦別人，帶貶義。

近 玲瓏剔透

英 **A slick and versatile person.** Referes to a person with verbal skills or hand dexterity, who accomplishes tasks with efficiency and grace. However, it is usually has a pejorative connotation referring to the indiscreetness or frivolousness of that person.

近 (a) smooth operator

158 口は災いの元* 6級

日解與用法 不用意な発言が原因で誤解を招いたり、恨みを買ったりして自分に思わぬ災難をもたらす。うかつに物を言わぬように、言葉遣いは十分に慎むべきだ、という戒め。

近義詞 禍は口より出ず 4級　口は禍の門 3級

漢 嘴是災禍的原因。講話口無遮攔往往失言賈禍。比喻說話要萬分謹慎。

近 禍從口出；是非只為多開口；口是禍之門，舌是斬身刀

英 **The mouth is the cause of calamity.** Better the foot slip than the tongue. Let not your tongue cut your throat.

近 Loose lips sink ships.; (A) word spoken is past recalling.; (A) closed mouth catches no flies.; Least said soonest mended.; Birds are entangled by their feet, and men by their tongues.

159 苦しい時の神頼み* 6級

日解與用法 信仰のない者が、苦しい時にだけ助けを求め神仏に祈ること。ふだん知らん顔をしている者が、自分が困った時にだけ他人に頼ろうとすることをいう。

近義詞 叶わぬ時の神叩き 4級　せつない時の神頼み 4級

漢 平時不信神的人，遇到困難才來求神保佑。意指平時對別人不聞不問，遇有急難需要幫助時才去懇求人。

近 平時不燒香，臨時抱佛腳（急來抱佛腳）；無事不登三寶殿；散兵坑裡沒有無神論者

英 **Invoke God's blessing only in time of distress**; Fig. One is apt to seek someone's help only when danger arises, whereas in a happy life, little attention is paid to them.

近 There are no atheists in foxholes.; Man's extremity is God's opportunity.

160 車の両輪 6級

日解與用法 車軸両側の二つの車輪。揃わないと役に立たないことから、二つのうち、どちらを欠いても成り立たないほど密接な関係にあることの喩え。

近義詞 鳥の両翼 5級　唇歯輔車 3級

漢 如車之雙輪，鳥之兩翼，兩者關係密切，相輔相成缺一不可。

近 輔車骨齒；骨齒相依

英 (like) **The two wheels on an axle**, which make everything roll. Fig. You can't have one without the other, they are inextricably linked and cannot be separated as an important driving forces. To work together as a single entity.

近 like peas and carrots; Two halves make a whole.

161 鶏口となるも牛後となるなかれ 6級

日解與用法 **牛の尻**(大きな組織の下っ端)**より鶏の口**(小さな組織のトップ)**になれ。** 大集団の低い地位に留まってこき使われるよりも、小集団の先頭に立って組織を引っ張った方がよい、ということの喩え。中国の古典に由来。

近義詞 鯛の尾より鰯の頭 3級 芋頭でも頭は頭 3級

漢 寧願做雞嘴而不願做牛臀。比喻寧可在小組織內當領導者，也不要在大組織內聽人支配。

近 寧為雞首，不為牛後

英 **Better to be a chicken's beak than an ox's rump.** (originated from a Chinese saying) Fig. It is better to be at the top of a small group than to be a unimportant staff member in a prestigious one. In other words, it's better to hold a high, worthwhile position in a small company than to hold a low position at a large one.

近 Better be the head of a dog than the tail of a lion.; Better a big fish in a little puddle than a little fish in a big puddle.; I had rather be first in a village than second at Rome.

162 芸は身を助ける * 6級

日解與用法 道楽として身につけた**芸**が思わぬところで**役に立つ**。財産や名声はなくなることがあっても、一度覚えた芸や技能は身につき、いざというときに生計を立てることもできるということの喩え。

近義詞 つぶしが利く 4級 手に職をつける

漢 比喻技藝可以幫助自己，總有派上用場的一天。財富名望可能有失去的時候，然而擁有一藝在手，隨時隨地隨身可用，受用無窮，特別是面對困境時。勉人必須具備一技之長。

近 家財萬貫不如一技在身；賜子千金不如賜子一藝；荒年餓不死手藝人

英 **If you have a** marketable **skill, you could very well need it** in case of emergency in the future. Learning something will never end up wasted, one day it may come in handy.

近 An occupation is as good as land.

163 怪我の功名 * 6級

日解與用法 **失敗が**思いがけなくも**手柄を立てる結果になること。**間違ってしたことや何気なくしたことが偶然にも良い結果をもたらすことの喩え。

近義詞 まぐれ当たり、怪我勝ち

漢 弄錯反而立功。比喻無意中犯了錯後居然還獲得意外的成效，或形容不經意的行動卻僥倖得到好結果。

近 歪打正著；無心插柳柳成蔭

英 **An accidental achievement from a failure.** a lucky break, a lucky mistake; a happy accident; Fig. Accidents change things for the better or bears unexpected fruit.

近 (just) by a fluke; by dumb luck; come out smelling like a rose

164 喧嘩両成敗* ⑥級

日解與用法 **喧嘩をした者は**、どんな言い分があっても、その良し悪しを問わず、**双方とも悪いとして両方処罰する**こと。公平な裁きとは言えないが、日本の中世武家の法令であった。「成敗」とは、処罰という意味。

近義詞 相手のない喧嘩はできぬ ④級

漢 爭吵打架雙方都有責任，不問情由，雙方都要懲罰。為中世時期武士的定律。

近 有理三扁擔，無理扁擔三

英 **When two quarrel, both** are in the wrong and **have to be punished** (as a decree of the Shogunate in middle ages); Fig. An argument is never only one person's fault, both have to share the blame for quarrel.

近 It takes two to make a quarrel.; It takes two to tango.; When two quarrel, both are in the wrong.

165 後悔先に立たず ⑥級

日解與用法 **先に悔いることはできない**。過ぎ去ってしまったことを悔やんでも取り返しがつかないのだから、後で悔やまなくても良いように、行動する前に十分考えなさいという教え。

近義詞 後悔臍を噛む ④級

漢 凡事不可能早先悔恨。比喻「悔不當初」無濟於事，因此事前宜慎重行事。

近 後悔莫及，噬臍莫及

英 **Repentance never comes beforehand**; Fig. Being wise after the event is too late, therefore, behave with careful forethought to avoid regretting it later.

近 It is no use crying over spilt milk.; Repentance is nothing but mockery when it comes too late.

166 紺屋の白袴 ⑥級

日解與用法 **紺屋なのに白い袴を穿いている**のは、染める仕事に追われて、自分の袴を染める暇がないのだろう、と揶揄していう。転じて、他人のためにばかり働いて、自分のことに手が回らないことを言う。

近義詞 大工の掘っ立て ④級　髪結いの乱れ髪 ④級

漢 藍染工坊的人給別人染衣服自己卻穿白褲。比喻為別人辛苦無暇照顧自己。

近 為人作嫁

英 **The dyer wears the colorless trousers.** Fig. This saying implies some professionals don't apply their skills for their direct use or for those closest to them because they are so anxious to make every penny they can out of his trade.

近 The shoemaker's children go barefoot.; Who is worse shod than shoemaker's wife?; The tailor's wife is the worst clad.

167 呉越同舟 _{6級}

167 呉越同舟 ⬛6級

日解與用法 敵同士であった**呉国と越国の人々が同じ船に乗り合わせた**時に、暴風に遭い、互いに助け合ったという故事から、仲の悪い者同士が同じ場所に居合わせること。また、敵味方が共通の利害のために協力することの喩え。中国の成語に由来。

近義詞 同舟相救う ⬛4級

漢 吳國人和越國人在暴風雨中同船，齊心合力，度過難關。比喻兩方在患難時捐棄前嫌，化敵為友，化干戈為玉帛，團結互助。

近 吳越同舟；同舟共濟；同甘共苦；休戚與共；唇亡齒寒

英 Bitter enemies in the same boat (**Wu and Yue** were fated rivals in ancient China, according to legend, found themselves **in the same boat** while caught up in the storm, and were forced to bury the hatchet and cooperate to survive) Fig. A common danger will sometimes draw even enemies to work together.

近 Woes unite foes.; While the thunder lasted, two bad men were friends.; Adversity makes strange bedfellows.

---

168 故郷へ錦を飾る ⬛6級

日解與用法 高価な**絹織物で身を着飾**って、胸を張って**故郷に帰る**意。立身出世した者が、晴れがましく故郷へ帰ること。

近義詞 錦を着て故郷に帰る ⬛4級

漢 穿着錦緞衣服回到家鄉，形容人功成名就後榮耀返鄉。

近 衣錦還鄉

英 **To return to one's hometown attired in brocade**, to return home after making good or after one's success.

近 to return to one's hometown in one's glory/in triumph

---

169 虎穴に入らずんば虎児を得ず ⬛6級

日解與用法 虎の子を捕らえるためには、虎の棲む穴に入らねばならない。思い切って冒険しない限り、大きな成功や成果を手に入れることはできないという喩え。中国の成語に由来。

近義詞 枝先に行かねば熟柿は食えぬ ⬛3級

漢 不進老虎窩，怎能捉到小老虎？比喻不深入險境，不經歷艱難，就不能獲取勝利成功。

近 不入虎穴，焉得虎子

英 **You cannot catch the tiger cub without entering the tiger's lair.** (comes from a Chinese proverb) Fig. He who is not courageous enough to take risks will accomplish nothing in life. Who dares wins. You can't achieve anything if you don't try.

近 Nothing ventured, nothing gained.; No guts, no glory.; He who would search for pearls must dive below.

170 子は鎹 [6級]

日解與用法 子供は夫婦の仲を和やかに繋ぎとめてくれるものだという喩え。「鎹」とは、二本の材木を繋ぎとめるために打ち込む、両端の曲がった「コ」の字形の金属製釘のこと。

近義詞 縁の切れ目は子で繋ぐ [4級] 子は縁つなぎ [4級]

漢 孩子就像一根 U 形釘一樣，把夫妻牽絆在一起。比喻兒女能填補父母間尷尬的間隙而縮短距離。「鎹」是一種兩端彎曲的金屬製固定鉤環。

近 孩子是夫妻間的紐帶

英 **Children are like a clamp.** Generally taken to imply that children play a role of a buffer in the conflict between couple. Children bridge the gap between the parents. Children are the bond that keeps the parents together.

近 (A) child is the pledge of affection.

171 転んでもただでは起きぬ [6級]

日解與用法 転んでもそのまま何もしないで立ち上がることはせず、必ずそこで何かを拾って起き上がるという意から、どんな場合にも利益を得ようとすること。抜け目がなく、貪欲な人や根性のある人を喩える。

近義詞 倒れても土を掴む [4級] こけても砂 [4級]

漢 即使是跌倒了，不會空著手站起來。比喻就算失敗，能撈則撈，總要得些好處。意指絕不輕易放過任何機會的貪婪的人，或暗指一個「有種」的人。

近 雁過拔毛；跌倒也要抓一把沙

英 **Even though one tumbles, one will get up with something that comes to his/her hands**; Fig. A person with guts and greed takes advantage of all the opportunities that come his/her way.

近 All is fish that comes to net./All's grist that comes to the mill.

172 コロンブスの卵 [6級]

日解與用法 新大陸の発見は誰にでもできると批判されたコロンブスが、卵を立てることを試みさせ、一人もできなかった後に卵の尻をつぶして立てて見せたという逸話から、一見誰でもできそうな簡単なことでも、最初に行うのは難しいということ。物事を解決する意外な方法の喩えにも使う。

近義詞 --

漢 哥倫布的難蛋。源自哥倫布豎立難蛋以說服哄笑他發現新大陸壯舉的人。他說明道：做任何事情看似簡單，但開頭都比較困難。

近 萬事起頭難

英 **An egg of Columbus**; Fig. The most difficult part of accomplishing something is getting started. Advocated by Columbus who used an egg to explain that people ususably take the solution for granted after the problem has been solved by others.

近 The first step is always the hardest.; All things are difficult before they are easy.

173 言語道断 ⁶級
（ごんごどうだん）

日解與用法 **言葉で言い表すことができないほどひどいこと、とんでもないこと。**
「言語」は言葉に出して言う、「道断」は言い表すことが絶えること。
仏教語で、仏教の真理や悟りの境地は、言葉で言い表して説明することが出来ないという意から。現在では悪い事柄を指すことが多い。

近義詞 沙汰の限り ³級　もってのほか

🈶 沒辦法用詞語來形容。大多指別人言行可惡已極或某一事物極其荒謬絕倫。

近 無可名狀；豈有此理

🇬🇧 **Too preposterous, too execrable, or too outrageous** to describe; Fig. How can this be so? Commonly used as a conventional reply to absurd or inexcusable behavior.

近 No way! That's out of the question!

174 先んずれば人を制す* ⁶級
（さきんずればひとをせいす）

日解與用法 何事も**先手を打つ**ことで、**相手を抑える**ことができる。人よりも先に行動すれば、断然有利な立場に立つことができるということ。出典は『史記』。

近義詞 先手必勝 ⁶級　早い者勝ち ⁴級　先手が万手 ⁴級

🈶 在對手沒有準備好的時候，**先動手發制人、可占優勢**。源自『史記』。

近 先下手為強，後下手遭殃；捷足先登

🇬🇧 **Who gets a head start controls others.** Fig. If you take the initiative, you are ahead of the rest and have an advantage. The expression is borrowed from the Chinese historical books "Shih-ji".

近 First come first served.; First up, best dressed.; The first blow is half the battle.; The first in the boat has the choice of oars.; He that runs fastest gets the ring.

175 匙を投げる ⁶級
（さじをなげる）

日解與用法 もう治療法がない、と医者が薬を調合するための**匙を投げ出し**、患者を見放すこと。努力しても好転する見込みがない、と手を引いて諦めることの喩え。

近義詞 見切りをつける ⁶級

🈶 病人已病入膏肓，醫生見病情無法好轉就放棄治療，**將調藥的藥匙丟在一遭**。比喻事態已經嚴重到無法挽救的地步，而放棄一切嘗試。

近 撒手不管；束手無策

🇬🇧 **To toss the medicine spoon** to signal that the doctor is going to abandon therapy. Fig. To quit or give up in despair.

近 pull the plug; throw in the towel

176 山椒は小粒でもぴりりと辛い _{6級}

日解與用法 山椒の実は小粒ながら、ぴりっとした辛みを持つことから、見かけは小柄でも才知に優れていて侮ることができない人をいう。

近義詞 小さくとも針は呑まれぬ _{4級}

漢 小粒的花椒又辣又嗆很起作用。比喻身軀矮小外表雖不引人注目，實際人小志大頭腦精明，不容輕侮。

近 秤錘雖小壓千斤

英 **A grain of *Sansho* (Japanese peppers) is pretty hot and spicy, though very small in size**; Fig. A phrase suggests that size isn't the only token of strength or ability. Despite being small in size, a person is too brilliant and ambitious to be trifled with.

近 A little body often harbors a great soul.; Good things come in small packages.

177 三度目の正直 _{6級}

日解與用法 勝負などで一回目、二回目はあてにならぬ、**三回目なら確実**ということ。また、二度の失敗の後にもめげずに再挑戦する時や、二度の失敗の後に期待通りに成功した時の形容に使う。

近義詞 三度目は定の目 _{4級}

漢 成事總在第三次。鼓勵人萬事成功於再三嘗試，一兩次的失敗第三次必能成功。也用於描述遭兩次失敗後第三次終於成功時的心境。

近 三次為定

英 **Things will turn out for the best the third time**; The belief that the third time something is attempted is more likely to succeed than the previous two. It is also used as third time is a good-luck charm, spoken just before trying something for the third time; after two failures fortune will be more incline to favor you.

近 Third time lucky.; Third time is a charm.; The third time pays for all.; All things thrive but thrice.

178 自画自賛 _{6級}

日解與用法 自分の描いた絵に自分で賛 (詩や文章) を添える。転じて、自分のことを褒め讃える意。

近義詞 手前味噌 _{6級}

漢 自己稱讚自己的畫好。比喻自我吹噓。

近 老王賣瓜，自賣自誇；賣瓜的說瓜甜；自吹自擂；自鳴得意

英 **To brag about one's own painting**; Fig. To praise or promote oneself; To call attention to one's abilities or achievements; To pat oneself on the back.

近 Every potter praises his own pot.; sing one's own praises.; Every peddler praises his own needles.; blow one's own trumpet; toot one's own horn

179 自業自得 _{6級}

日解與用法 自分の業 (行為) の報いを自分自身が受けること。つまり、自分がした悪い行いの報いが自分の身に返る、種を蒔いたからには刈り取らなければならないことの喩え。

近義詞 因果応報 _{6級}　爾に出ずるものは爾に反る _{4級}　自縄自縛 _{4級}

漢 自己做了蠢事壞事的後果自己承擔，罪有應得。形容只要造因，就得面對果報。

近 自作自受；自食其果；作繭自縛；咎由自取；種瓜得瓜，種豆得豆

英 You have to suffer the consequences of what you do. Said that you must live with the consequences of your deeds, good or bad, will repay you in kind.

近 As you sow, so shall you reap.; As you make your bed, so you must lie on it.; The chickens come home to roost.; He that mischief hatches mischief catches.

180 地獄で仏 _{6級}

日解與用法 地獄で、慈悲深い仏に会えば嬉しく有難い。困り果てている時に、思わぬ助けを得ることの喩え。

近義詞 闇夜に提灯 _{4級}　闇夜の灯火 _{4級}　日照りに雨 _{4級}

漢 似在地獄遇到佛陀。比喻在危急苦難的時候得到意外的援助，獲得生路。

近 久旱逢甘雨，他鄉遇故知；及時甘霖；絕路逢生

英 Like **meeting the Buddha in Hell**. Fig. Be very lucky to get help in one's hour of need; Something wanted or needed that comes timely and unexpectedly, as if is sent by God.

近 meet a good Samaritan in disastrous circumstances

181 地震雷火事親父 _{6級}

日解與用法 世の中で恐れられているものを順に並べて、**地震、雷、火事の次に親父が怖い**という。昔の家父長制のもとでの親父の威厳を現す言葉。

近義詞 --

漢 世上的**四大怕：地震、打雷、火災、老爸**。描繪不久以前的日本封建式的家長制度下父親的威嚴，如同地震，打雷，火災的可怕。

近 --

英 **Earthquakes, thunderbolts, fires, and fathers**: brings to mind four things named in ascending order of powers in Japan, not that long ago. The father is the most respected and intimidating figure in the family, therefore, the father used to be thought as the most feared as much as the worst natural disasters.

近 Love and fear. Everything the father of a family says must inspire one or the other. (by Joseph Joubert)

182 尻尾を掴む ⑥級

日解與用法 化けた狐や狸**の尻尾を掴んで**正体を暴く意。他人のごまかしや悪事の証拠などを押さえる、また他人の弱点や秘密を見抜くことの喩え。

近義詞 弱みを握る ⑤級

漢 似**抓到**狐狸的尾巴一樣。意指抓到別人作假或穢行的把柄，看穿他人的弱點，秘密或真面目。

近 抓小辮子

英 **To clutch the tail in one's hands**; Fig. To catch someone out in a fraud or wrongdoing; To get hold of a weak point or damaging, confidential information about someone.

近 reveal people's true colors; get something on someone

183 四面楚歌 ⑥級

日解與用法 劉邦の漢軍に包囲された楚の項羽が、夜更けに**四面の漢軍が楚の歌を歌う**のを聞き、楚の民がすでに漢軍に降伏したと思い、戦意を失ったという故事から、周囲がすべて敵や反対者で、孤立無援である状況をいう。

近義詞 孤立無援 ⑥級　八方ふさがり ⑤級

漢 被劉邦的漢軍包圍在垓下的項羽，半夜聽見四周漢軍的軍營唱起楚歌，感覺吃驚絕望而失去戰意。形容陷入四面受敵，孤立無援的窘迫境地。

近 四面楚歌；孤立無援；腹背受敵；走投無路

英 **Hearing the Chu Danasty songs from all sides of the Han's barracks** (the leader of Chu troops instantly lost his will to fight just by knowing that they were isolated and cut off from outside aid); Fig. Be assailed from all sides; Be left unsupported; Be completely isolated and feel like the whole world is against you.

近 (be) left high and dry; (be) caught in the crossfire

184 弱肉強食 ⑥級

日解與用法 **弱者の肉を強者が食べる**ことから、弱い者の犠牲によって強い者が繁栄することの喩え。中国の成句に由来する表現。

近義詞 優勝劣敗 ④級

漢 強者吞食弱者，比喻強者欺凌吞併弱者。

近 弱肉強食；以強淩弱；大魚吃小魚，小魚吃蝦米

英 **The weak are the prey of the strong**; (borrowed from a Chinese proverb); Fig. The law of the jungle; The survival of the fittest; The weak are always trampled by the powerful.

近 Big fish eat little fish.; The weakest goes to the wall.; The great ones eat up the little ones.

185 尻切れトンボ 6級

日解與用法 **尻(尾)の切れたトンボ**。トンボの尾が切れると飛べなくなる。物事が中途で途切れて後が続かない、投げ出して完結しないことをいう。語源は「蜻蛉草履」という昔からの履物からきているといわれている。鼻緒の先をトンボの翅のような形に結び、踵に当たる部分がない短い草履。

近義詞 中途半端 5級

漢 像被切掉尾巴的蜻蜓。比喻沒定性見異思遷的人，做事半途而廢，不能貫徹始終。據說句中的「トンボ」並非指昆蟲的蜻蛉，而是一種稱為「トンボ草履」沒有後跟的草鞋。

近 有頭無尾；有始無終；虎頭蛇尾；半途而廢；不了了之

英 **Like a damaged (in the rear) dragonfly**; Fig. A sudden and abrupt end; Refers to a person who lacks the power to stick to a subject and fails to carry something through to the end; Things left unsettled. Some say that *tombo* is not a term referring to dragonfly but indicating Japanese sandals (its design look alike).

近 give up halfway; drop by the wayside

186 尻に火が付く 6級

日解與用法 **尻に火が付いた**ほどに切羽詰まった状況や、追い詰められた状態を指す。または、危険が身近に迫って当事者は落ち着いていられない様子をいう。

近義詞 足下に火が付く 4級　頭から火が付く 4級　眉に火が付く 4級　焦眉の急 3級

漢 火快燒到屁股。比喻事到眼前，情勢非常急迫。

近 火燒眉毛；燃眉之急；迫在眉睫；刻不容緩

英 **Extremely sudden as fire singes one's rear end**; Fig. In a perilous state and something must be done to solve a burning issue; To call for desperate measures at a critical moment; It is a common taunt when someone is in imminent danger that demands immediate attention.

近 The pressure is on.; (be) at a crisis point

187 心機一転 6級

日解與用法 あることをきっかけにして、心持ちがすっかり変わること。また、気持ちを切り替えることによって、良い方向へ、明るい方向へと変化すること。「心機」は**心の動き、気持ち**。「一転」は**がらりと変わる**こと。

近義詞 一念発起 6級　気分一新 6級

漢 因為某個因素，心情為之一變。意指改變思維心態後，心情為之一振，重獲新生，步往好的局面。

近 洗心革面；脫胎換骨

英 **Totally change one's mindset** after some event and start over again; Fig. To make a completely new start by changing one's attitude and behave in a better way.

近 turn over a new leaf

188 雀百まで踊り忘れず* 6級

日解與用法 ぴょんと飛び跳ねる**雀は、年をとっても跳ねる仕草をする。**同じ様に、人が幼い時に身につけた習慣や若い時に覚えた道楽は、生涯抜けきれない。通常、良い習慣については使わない。

近義詞 病は治るが癖は治らぬ 4級　噛む馬はしまいまで噛む 3級

漢 麻雀活到百歲也不忘蹦跳。幼時的癖好或習慣終生難改。通常指不好的嗜好。

近 習與性成；江山易改，本性難移；稟性難移；積習難改

英 **A sparrow never forgets how to dance until hundred.** Fig. Everything you acquired in childhood (usually bad things) stays with you during your whole life. Old habits die hard.

近 What is learnt in the cradle lasts to the tomb.; What the colt learns in youth he continues in old age.; As the twig is bent, so is the tree inclined.; Habit is second nature.

189 全ての道はローマに通ず 6級

日解與用法 ローマ帝国の全盛期には、**世界各地からの道がローマに通じていたこ**とから、方法や手段は異なっても目指す目標は同じであることの喩え。言い換えれば、目的を達成するのに、方法や手段は何通りもあるという。英語に由来する表現。

近義詞 百川海に朝す 3級

漢 每條途徑都抵達羅馬。比喻無論採用什麼方法，得到的效果或目標相同。源自英文名言。

近 條條大路通羅馬；殊途同歸；百川歸海

英 **All paths lead to Roman Empire.** (borrowed from an English adage). It means that different paths can take one to the same goal, one may reach the same goal by different means.

近 All roads lead to Rome.

190 青天の霹靂 6級

日解與用法 雲ひとつない**青く晴れ渡った空に、**何の前触れもなく、**いきなり雷鳴が起**こること。予期しない衝撃的な事件や、不測の事態が突然生じることをいう。

近義詞 寝耳に水 4級　藪から棒* 6級

漢 陽光普照的晴朗天氣裡突然響雷。比喻發生出人意料或令人震驚的事件。

近 晴天霹靂

英 Totally **unforeseen lightning or thunder from a cloudless blue sky**; Fig. Something completely unexpected that surprises you very much.

近 a bolt from the blue / a bolt out of the blue; out of the blue / out of a clear blue sky

191 背に腹は代えられぬ* 6級

日解與用法 腹を背中の代わりにすることはできない。同じ体の一部ではあっても、どちらか一方しか守れない時は、背を犠牲にしても大切な腹は守らなくてはならない。二者択一の情況では、大事な方を選択せざるを得ない。

近義詞 苦しい時は鼻をも削ぐ 4級

漢 腹部不能代替背脊，為了保護腹部不得已而犧牲脊背。比喻為了顧全大局必須犧牲次要的小節。兩利相權取其重。

近 棄卒保帥；斷尾求生；捨不得鞋子，套不住狼

英 You can't replace belly for back. Fig. Alludes to a situation about something you have to do not because you want to but necessity compels you. In other words, you cannot save an important thing without making some sacrifice.

近 Needs must when the devil drives.; Near is my coat, but nearer is my shirt.; You can't make an omelette without breaking eggs.

192 善は急げ* 6級

日解與用法 良いと思ったことは、躊躇せずただちに実行に移した方がよいという教え。

近義詞 思い立ったが吉日* 6級　旨い物は宵に食え 3級

漢 好事務急辦。比喻你若認為做某事是有益或合適的，則立即付諸行動。

近 兵貴神速；事不宜遲；從善如流

英 Be quick to do what you think is right. Fig. If it's worth doing, it's worth doing promptly. Don't wait to perform good deeds. A saying suggesting that we act on opportunities.

近 The tide must be taken when it comes.; Never put off till tomorrow what you can do today.

193 千里の道も一歩より始まる* 6級

日解與用法 千里もある遠い道のりも、まず一歩を踏み出すことから始まる。大事業も、まず手近なところから着実に努力を重ねていけば成功するという教え。「千里の道も一歩から」、「千里の行も足下より始まる」ともいう。中国の古典に由来。

近義詞 高きに登るには卑きよりす 3級

漢 千里的路程也得從眼前的一小步走起。比喻事情的成功，是從小到大逐漸積累起來的，絕無一步登天的道理。任何遠大的目標，得從細微的小事情做起。勸人腳踏實地，不能急功近利，倉促求成。

近 千里之行，始於足下；一步一腳印；萬丈高樓平地起；登高必自卑，行遠必自邇；砌牆先打基，吃蛋先養難

英 A journey of a thousand miles begins with taking the first step. (originated in a Chinese saying) Fig. If you want to get far, you must start slowly from up close. A large, successful business was very small or simple when it began.

近 He who would climb the ladder must begin at the bottom.; Great/Mighty oaks from little acorns grow.

194 対岸の火事 6級

日解與用法 川向こうの火事はこちらの岸まで燃え移る心配がない。どんな重大な問題であっても、利害関係がなく見ているだけの人間にとっては、痛くも痒くもないということをいう。

近義詞 川向こうの火事 3級　川向かいの喧嘩 3級

漢 對岸的火災。反正火勢不會延燒過岸而冷眼旁觀。形容置身事外的態度。因事不干己不痛不癢，對他人的問題漠不關心。

近 隔岸觀火；袖手旁觀

英 Fire on the opposite shore of the river; Fig. To distance oneself from the case or to be apathetic to others' troubles as one knows it won't affect him/her; What happens elsewhere is a matter of indifference.

近 It is easy to bear the misfortunes of others.; It's no skin off my nose/teeth.; The comforter's head never aches.

195 太鼓判を捺す 6級

日解與用法 保証人として太鼓のように大きい判を押す。人の能力、事物の価値、品質の良さは絶対に間違いない、と確信をもって保証する意。

近義詞 折り紙をつける 6級　お墨付きを与える 4級

漢 蓋上大鼓一樣大的印章。意指對人或對物的品質拍胸脯下保證絕對沒問題。

近 打保票／打包票

英 To give the stamp (big as drum-size) of approval to someone or something; Strong recommendation, full endorsement; Vouch for someone's ability or something's quality without reservation.

近 vouch for (someone or something)

196 大山鳴動して鼠一匹 6級

日解與用法 大きい山が鳴り響き揺れ動くので、噴火でも起こるのかと思って見守れば、飛び出してきたのはたった一匹の鼠だった。「産気づいた山から生まれたのは鼠一匹」というラテン寓話由来の表現。大騒ぎしたわりに、結果は取るに足らないことの喩え。

近義詞 蛇が出そうで蚊も出ぬ 4級

漢 大山鳴動卻只跑出一隻耗子。源自拉丁語的寓言。形容聲勢浩大而結果卻讓人不如預期。或比喻為一些不足為奇的小事而過分誇張、驚怪。

近 雷聲大雨點小；大驚小怪；小題大作

英 The mountain has labored and brought forth a mouse. (originated from a Latin fable); Fig. A relatively small event exaggerated out of proportion to its actual significance; Big fuss, tiny result.

近 make much ado about nothing; much cry and little wool; (a) storm/tempest in a teacup

197 大は小を兼ねる 6級

日解與用法 大きいものは小さいものの代用として使える。小さいものより大きいものの方が使い道が広く、役に立つということを強調していう。

近義詞 大は小を叶える 4級

漢 大能兼小。意指大的東西可替代小的東西，即強調大的東西用途較廣泛。

近 寧大勿小

英 Larger (greater) also serves as a smaller (lesser); Fig. Better too big than too small; The bigger you have the better off you are; Simply a phrase to emphasize the larger is of wide use, it serves two or more functions simultaneously.

近 Bigger is always better.; The greater good.; Store is no sore.; Wide will wear, but narrow will tear.

---

198 宝の持ち腐れ 6級

日解與用法 宝を持っていながら、使い道を知らなかったり、出し惜しみをしたり、役立てずに腐らせてしまう意。価値のあるもの、才能や技能を持っていながら、それを十分活かしきれない・発揮できないでいること。

近義詞 筆筒の肥やし（ニュアンスはちょっと違う）5級

漢 空藏寶玉不知運用到最後腐朽掉了。比喻白白糟蹋好的東西，或擁有優秀的才能卻不能施展發揮。

近 捧著金碗要飯吃；空懷屠龍之技；英雄無用武之地

英 The hoarded treasure left unused is but trash; A concise way of saying unused treasure is a useless possession; Also refers to a waste of talent; To own something valuable without realizing it.

近 (A) book that remains shut, is but a block.; No possession, but use, is the only riches.; Better spent than spared.; (be) sitting on a goldmine

---

199 他山の石 6級

日解與用法 他の山から出た粗末な石でも、それを砥石に使えば自分の玉を磨くのに役立つ。転じて、自分より劣っている人の言行も自分の行いの参考や戒めになる。出典：中国の成句「他山の石、以て玉を攻むべし」。

近義詞 人の振り見て我が振り直せ* 6級　人こそ人の鏡 3級

漢 別的山上的石頭，可以作為礪石用來琢磨玉器。意指他人的行為或意見能夠幫助自己改正錯誤缺點或提供借鑒。

近 他山之石（可以攻玉）

英 Stones from the other mountains can be used as a whetstone to polish one's own gems; Fig. Other's behavior provides us with a great deal of food for thought; One should learn from other's shortcomings; To improve oneself by accepting criticism from outside (originated in a Chinese saying).

近 The dullness of the fool is the whetstone of the wits.; The fault of another is a good teacher.

200 多勢に無勢 ⑥級

日解與用法 多人数の敵に少人数で立ち向かっても勝ち目がないということ。数の多い相手には敵対しがたいという。

近義詞 衆寡敵せず ⑤級

漢 人多勢眾，人少的抵擋不過人多的群體。

近 寡不敵眾；好虎架不住一群狼

英 **The few are no match for the many.** Small numbers are no match for great numbers; To be hopelessly outnumbered by one's opponents; To fight against hopeless odds.

近 fight against longer odds; Providence is always on the side of the big battalions.

201 只より高いものは無い ⑥級

日解與用法 ただで物を貰うと、返礼に相応またはそれ以上の金がかかるし、頼みを聞かなくてはならないかも知れない、**結局は高くつく**ということ。また、世の中には、ただ飯はないという戒め。

近義詞 買うは貰うに勝る ③級

漢 沒有比免費還貴的東西。拿人禮物也得還禮，說不定還得應其要求，結果反而連本帶利。告誡人們「世上哪有白吃的午餐，任何事情都需要付出代價」

近 天下沒有白吃的午餐；吃人家的嘴軟，拿人家的手短

英 **Nothing costs as much as what is given to you for free.** Fig. If someone gives you something, they always expect you to do something in return. What looks like a good deal will end up costing you more in the long run. Everything has a price.

近 There is no such thing as a free lunch.; You don't get something for nothing.

202 旅の恥は掻き捨て* ⑥級

日解與用法 旅先には顔見知りもいないし、長く滞在するわけでもないので、普段ならしないような恥ずかしい言動も平気でするものだということ。知らない土地で分からないことは当然沢山あるから、結果的に恥をかくことも多くなる。恥ずかしがっても仕方がない、と開き直った思いを表す言葉でもある。

近義詞 --

漢 **出門旅遊，無所顧忌不怕出洋相**。比喻旅途中想玩得盡興，做些丟臉的事無所謂，心想反正沒有人認識你，回家不說也沒有人知道。亦可解釋為到異國他鄉旅遊，因人地生疏不熟悉的事太多，難免出醜，但也無可奈何。

近 恬不知恥

英 **When traveling, cast off your sense of shame.** Most people do "things" on a far journey that they normaly wouldn't do in their own hometown, they believe nothing will come back to trouble them as long as all exploits during the tour are not discussed with anyone. Possibly interpreted as one has no other alternative to make a fool of oneself when visiting an unfamiliar place.

近 What happens on tour stays on tour.; What happens in Vegas stays in Vegas.

た行

203 旅は道連れ世は情け* [6級]

日解與用法 **旅には同行者**がいると心強く感じられるように、この**世の中**を渡っていくには互いに支え合う**人情や思いやり**が大切だということ。

近義詞 よき道連れは里程を縮める [4級]　旅は心、世は情け [4級]

漢 旅行要有旅伴互相照應也能增加樂趣。處世要靠人情互相關照扶持，就能安心地渡日。

近 行要好伴，住要好鄰；旅途有好伴，路遙不覺遠

英 **We need companions in a trip, we need compassion on our life-long journey.** Thought as a traditional modus operandi in Japan. It is reassuring to have a pleasant companion when traveling, and it is important to associate with people and care for each other throughout life.

近 Good company on the road is the shortest cut.; An agreeable companion on the road is as good as a coach.; Joy shared is joy doubled; sorrow shared is sorrow halved.

204 玉に瑕 [6級]

日解與用法 **宝玉の表面にできた瑕**。転じて、最上のものの中にある小さな欠点のことを指す。それさえなければ完璧なのに、惜しいことにわずかながら欠点があることを強調する言葉。

近義詞 白璧の微瑕 [4級]

漢 潔白的璧玉上的小瑕疵。比喻很好的人或事有小缺點，帶有「美中不足」惋惜的意味。

近 白圭之玷；白璧微瑕

英 **Flaw in the jade**; Fig. A slight but irritating flaw that detracts from value or completeness (of a person or thing); Usually the speaker feels sorry for the fact that the blemish spoils the whole thing.

近 fly in the ointment; A good garden may have some weeds. (Thomas Fuller)

205 短気は損気* [6級]

日解與用法 **辛抱ができず、すぐ癇癪を起こしたりすると、人間関係がこじれるため、結局自分の損になる**ことが多い。短気を起こすな、という戒めの言葉。

近義詞 急いては事を仕損じる* [6級]　癇癪持ちの事破り [3級]

漢 形容脾氣急躁易怒的人容易與人起衝突誤事。勸人心平氣和，否則氣大傷身。

近 小不忍，則亂大謀

英 **A short temper brings damage or loss.** Fig. This is a warning not to get hotheaded. A person who loses one's temper quickly provokes a conflict, besides, when one's temper goes out of control, it can have serious consequences for relationships, health, and state of mind.

近 Anger and haste hinder good counsel.; Don't cut off your nose to spite your face.; He who is slow to anger has great understanding. But he who is quick-tempered exalts folly. (Bible); Anger punishes itself.

206 提灯に釣鐘* 6級

日解與用法 提灯と釣鐘はともに吊り下げて用いるもので、形も似ているが、軽重の差は甚だしく大きく、比べ物にならない。物事の釣り合いが取れないことを指す。縁談の話で、両家の家柄の不釣り合いの喩えに用いる。

近義詞 瓢箪に釣鐘 4級　箸に虹梁 4級

漢 燈籠跟吊鐘。兩個的外形乍看雖然相似都是提著用的東西，其實輕重根本不一樣。比喻兩者極不匹配，通常指男女雙方家世背景相差懸殊。

英 A hanging **paper lantern with temple bell**, two common items in old Japan, as an example of two things which look similar but do not go together; Fig. Said about an ill-assorted pair, an ill-matched couple or families that are far apart in terms of social status.

近 門不當戶不對；癩蛤蟆想吃天鵝肉

近 one who doesn't marry one's match

207 沈黙は金、雄弁は銀 6級

日解與用法 何も語らず**黙っていること**は、巧みによどみなく**話すことよりも大切**であるということ。場合によって口をきかぬが最上の分別で、沈黙の方が雄弁より説得力があるかも知れない。英語由来の表現。

近義詞 言わぬは言うに勝る 3級

漢 沉默是金、雄辯是銀。源自英語的成語。意指沉默的價值比雄辯來得高。多說不如不說，沉默是上策，善辯是下策。

英 **Silence is golden, eloquence is silver** (a direct translation of the English proverb); Fig. Saying nothing is better, eloquent words can be less valuable than no words as discretion counts in some cases.

近 沉默是金、善辯是銀

近 Speech is silver, silence is golden.; If a word be worth one shekel, silence is worth two.

208 爪に火を点す* 6級

日解與用法 ろうそくの代わりに切った爪に火を点して明かりにする。ひどくけちなこと、また、極端に倹約すること。

近義詞 財布の紐を締める 5級

漢 用剪下的指甲點火充蠟燭。比喻吝嗇透頂（捨不得買蠟燭）或非常節省（窮得買不起蠟燭）。

英 Very stingy or thrifty; Fig. One who is very reluctant to spend money or one who pinches pennies or one who lives on very little money even **burning one's fingernail parings** for heat or light.

近 一毛不拔；省吃儉用

近 skin a flint; skin a flea for its hide; scrimp and save; pinch and scrape

79

209 手前味噌 ⁶級

日解與用法 **自分の家で作った味噌**の味を大げさに自慢する意。自分や身内のした
ことを誇ること。かつて、各家庭で味噌を作り、良い味を出すために
工夫を凝らしていたことから。

近義詞 自画自賛 ⁶級

漢 自己炫耀**自己家做的味噌好**。比喻自
己誇耀自己或親人所做的事。以前的
日本家庭自己調製味噌，每家有獨特
的做法，味道也各有千秋。

近 老王賣瓜，自賣自誇；自吹自擂；沾
沾自喜

英 To brag about one's **homemade soybean paste** (A
traditional Japanese ingredient produced by ferment-
ing soybeans); Fig. A boast of one's own fine qualities
to make oneself feel special; Being ten feet tall about
one's achievements.

近 Every potter praises his own pot.; sing one's own
praises; blow one's own trumpet; toot one's own horn;
All his geese are swans.

210 手も足も出ない ⁶級

日解與用法 **手も足も出せない。**自分の力が及ばず、どうすることもできず、困り果て
ている様子をいう。対処する方法がなく、手の施しようがないことの喩え。

近義詞 お手上げ ⁵級

漢 像**手腳伸不出去**一樣。比喻茫然不知
所措，毫無辦法。

近 束手無策；一籌莫展；無計可施

英 **Neither the hands nor the feet will move.**; Be unable
to do anything; Fig. Be at a loss what to do; Feeling
quite helpless.

近 (be) at one's wit's end; (be) at the end of one's tether;
have one's hands tied; have one's fate sealed

211 天は自ら助くる者を助く ⁶級

日解與用法 **天は努力する者を助ける。**他人を当てにせず、自ら道を切り開こうと
する者には、神の加護があるという意味。英語のことわざの訳語。

近義詞 人事を尽くして天命を待つ ⁵級

漢 **天助自助者。**人必先自助而後天助之。
意指想達到自己想要的結果，首先要靠
自己勤奮努力。源自英語成語。

近 天助自助者；盡人事聽天命；皇天不
負苦心人

英 **Heaven helps those who help themselves.** A popu-
lar motto that emphasizes the importance of self-
initiative. You cannot depend solely on divine help,
but must work yourself to get what you want (a direct
translation from the English proverb).

近 God helps those who help themselves.; Do the likeli-
est, and God will do the best.

212 遠くの親類より近くの他人 6級

日解與用法 いざという時には、**遠く離れて疎遠になった親戚より、近くに住む赤の他人**の方が頼りになるということ。だからこそ、普段から近所付き合いを大切にしておかなくてはならないという教え。

近義詞 遠くの一家より近くの隣* 4級　遠き親子より近き隣 4級

漢 遠親不如近鄰。意指當發生緊急事情時，與其拜託在遠方的親戚，倒不如找隔壁鄰居才可及時得到幫助，所以平時就要和鄰居們和諧相處，守望相助。

近 遠親不如近鄰；遠水不救近火

英 A relative afar is less helpful than a close neighbor. Fig. Take whatever help is on hand, rather than an estranged relative. A saying which is to remind you to get on well with your neighbors.

近 Better a neighbor nearby than a relative far away.; A near neighbor is better than a far-dwelling kinsman.

213 時は金なり 6級

日解與用法 一度過ぎてしまうと、二度と戻って来ない**時間は、お金と同じように貴重**なものであるから、無駄にしてはならない。時間を有効に使うべきだということの喩え。英語圏のことわざの訳語。

近義詞 一刻千金 4級　一寸の光陰軽んずべからず 3級

漢 時間就是金錢。意指時間和金錢一樣的重要，必須珍惜。源自英語成語。

近 一寸光陰一寸金，寸金難買寸光陰；一刻千金

英 Time is money. Fig. Time is valuable and should not be wasted. Nothing is more precious than time. Every second counts. It's a direct translation from the English proverb.

近 Time is money.

214 年寄りの冷や水* 6級

日解與用法 年寄りが強がって冷たい水を浴びたり、氷水を飲んだり、自分の年齢や体力を考えずに無茶なことをすることの喩え。高齢者に似つかわしくない振る舞いを戒めたり冷やかしたりして言う。

近義詞 年寄りの力 3級　老いの木登り 3級

漢 老人沖冷水(喝冷水)。意指老人家老當益壯，逞強學年輕人沖冷水或飲冰水，自認實習老人未老。含有諷刺老人家不服老，自不量力，不知自愛的語氣。

近 人老心不老；壽星吃砒霜；黄忠七十不服老；老馬展鬃

英 An elderly person bathing in cold water; Fig. Something that a person who is considered too old to attempt; To ridicule an old person who is doing something not befitting his/her age (a formerly widespread belief in Japan that drinking cold water or bathing in cold water makes elderly people cramp up and get sick).

近 An old sack wanteth much patching.; Act your age, not your shoe size.

215 隣の花は赤い ^{6級}

日解與用法 隣の垣に咲いている**花は、ひときわ赤く**美しく見える。他人のものは
何でもよく見えて、うらやましく思うことの喩え。足るを知らない者
は常に自分が持っている物や自分の境遇より、他人の物や他人の境遇
の方がよく見えてしまう。

近義詞 隣の芝生は青い ^{6級} 隣の糂汰味噌 ^{3級}

漢 羨慕隔壁院子開的花比較紅。用以指
永不知足的人，總覺得別人的東西、
別人的境況比自己的美好。

近 這山望著那山高；家花不如野花香；
隔壁人家飯菜香

英 **Flowers next door always appear to be red.** Fig. It
seems people are never satisfied with their own situation, they always think others have it better.

近 The grass is always greener on the other side (of the fence).;
The apples on the other side of the wall are the sweetest.

216 鳶が鷹を生む* ^{6級}

日解與用法 **平凡な親（鳶）から優秀な子（鷹）が生まれる。**鳶も鷹も同じタカ科
の猛禽類で、姿は似ているが、鳶を平凡な者、鷹を優れた者に喩えて
いる。動物の死骸や生ごみなどを食べる鳶の卑しいイメージと、鷹狩
りに使われる威厳のある鷹のイメージに由来すると思われる。聞く立
場によっては、ばかにされていると取られることもあるので、使用に
注意が必要。

近義詞 鳶が孔雀を生む ^{3級}

漢 黑鳶生出了老鷹。比喻平庸寒微人家
培養出了傑出的人物，凡人生貴子。
通常為褒義，但也可以用於帶貶義的
口氣，須留意使用。黑鳶與老鷹都屬
鷹科猛禽，外貌酷似。但因黑鳶常以
腐肉或垃圾為食，形象不如老鷹勇猛。
因此日人視黑鳶為平庸，視老鷹為卓
越的鳥類。

近 鴉窩裡出鳳凰 / 鴉巢生鳳 / 老鴰窩裡
出鳳凰；烏雞母生白雞卵

英 **A kite begets a hawk**; Fig. Said when a great person is
born to perfectly ordinary parents or a humble family.
This expression can be used either admiringly or deri-
sively. *Tobi* (kites) and *taka* (hawks) are similar birds of
prey in the family Accipitridae. Kites are stereotyped
as bad birds in Japan since they often seen foraging
dead rodents and garbage, yet eagles are thought of as
proficient hunters.

近 Black hens lay white eggs.

217 鳶に油揚げを攫われる 6級

日解與用法 自分のものになる筈のもの(油揚げ)を他人(鳶)に横合いからいきなり奪われること。ふいに横取りされて呆然としている様子にも使う。悠々と空に輪を描いて飛ぶ鳶が、獲物を見つけた時の素早い動作から由来する句。

近義詞 疾風迅雷 3級　電光石火 3級

漢 乗人不備時讓黑鳶刁走豆腐皮。比喻出其不意地讓自己本來可以拿到手的東西被搶走，一時之間不知所措。赤形容因吃驚而發愕的樣子。黑鳶在高空盤旋飛行尋覓食物，一旦發現獵物時即以迅雷不及掩耳的速度俯衝而下。

近 趁虛而入；猝不及防；措手不及；煮熟的鴨子飛了

英 **Have one's fried bean curd snatched away by a black kite**; Fig. To snatch something nice that someone is about to get from under his/her nose when he/she is not ready for it; Black kites are most often seen gliding on the sky as they search for food. They will swoop down suddenly to snatch any food that they find.

近 (be) caught unaware; (be) caught with your pants down; (be) caught off guard; (be) caught on the hop; (be) caught napping

218 虎の威を借る狐 6級

日解與用法 弱い狐が強い虎の威勢を借りて態度を大きくすること。他人の権勢を頼りに威張ること。影響力を持つ者の力に頼って偉そうに振舞う小人物を指す。出典は中国の四字熟語。

近義詞 笠に着て威張る 4級

漢 狐狸假借老虎的威勢。比喻沒有實力的人依仗別人的勢力欺壓人，也指藉著權威人士的權力作威作福的小人。

近 狐假虎威；狗仗人勢；仗勢欺人；驢蒙虎皮

英 **The fox exploits the tiger's ferocity** (originated in a Chinese adage); Fig. Someone who pretends to be greater than he truly is, intimidating people by flaunting one's powerful connections.

近 (a) donkey in the lion's skin; Clothes may disguise a fool, but his words will give him away.

219 泥棒を捕えて縄を綯う 6級

日解與用法 泥棒を捕まえてから慌てて縄をより合わせても、泥棒は逃げてしまう。事が起きてから慌てて準備して対処することの喩え。

近義詞 渇して井を穿つ 4級　火事後の火の用心 4級

漢 看到小偷後才開始結繩索。比喻事到臨頭才準備才採取措施，緩不濟急。

近 臨陣磨鎗；臨渴掘井；江心補漏

英 **To start making a rope after seeing a thief**; Fig. Fail to plan ahead or prepare on time; Be too late in taking steps to prevent a bad event; To take belated precautions after damage has occurred.

近 Shut the stable door after the horse has bolted.; Lock the barn door after the horse is stolen.; Have not thy cloak to make when it begins to rain.

220 生兵法は大怪我のもと ⑥級

日解與用法 **生半可に兵法(武術)を知った者**が、それに頼り軽々しく事を行うのは**大怪我の原因**となる。玄人ぶって生かじりの知識や技能に頼ると、かえって失敗することの喩え。

近義詞 生兵法は知らぬに劣る ④級

漢 只知道一點兵法或武術就自以為是的人，往往容易受重傷。比喻一知半解，半生不熟的東西反而有害無益。一招半式(闖江湖)比未練過功夫還糟。

近 略知毛皮反而誤事

英 Shallow, simple-minded military tactics can cause great injury; Fig. If you only know a little about something, you may feel you are qualified to make judgements, but in fact, you are not.

近 A little knowledge is a dangerous thing.

---

221 逃がした魚は大きい ⑥級

日解與用法 **小さな魚でも、釣り落とすと大きく思えてくる。**手に入れ損なったものは、口惜しい気持ちが増幅されて、実際よりも大きく立派に思えてくるものだということの喩え。

近義詞 釣り落した魚は大きい ⑥級　逃げた鯰は大きく見える ④級

漢 逃掉的魚都是大的。即使魚根本不大，漏網或沒有抓到的魚都感覺較大較好。錯失了快要到手的東西，必定是一種又遺憾又不甘心的滋味。

近 跑了的魚大；得不到的總是最好的

英 A fish that dropped off the hook seems bigger than it is. A fisherman is apt to think that the fish that got away was very big and exaggerated the size of it. Fig. Regret magnifies the loss. One may think that it's a shame to let such an opportunity just pass.

近 The one that got away (is always bigger).; You should have seen the one that got away!

---

222 憎まれっ子世にはばかる* ⑥級

日解與用法 皆から**嫌われる**可愛げのない**人(子供)ほど**、世の中をうまく渡って行き、威勢を振るうということ。

近義詞 雑草は早く伸びる ②級　渋柿の長持ち ②級

漢 遭人嫌的人(孩子)盛氣凌人，放肆囂張。意指令人討厭憎惡的人物反而在社會中得勢。

近 小人得志，(君子道消)；瓦釜雷鳴

英 A hated kid runs wild and acts big throughout the world. Fig. Something that you say to a hated figure who has great power and behaves as he/she likes.

近 Ill weeds grow apace.; The more knave, the better luck.; The devil's children have the devil's luck.; The devil looks after his own.

223 二束三文 _{6級}

日解與用法 二束もあるのに三文 (草履の値段) というわずかな値打ちしかない意
から、数量が多くても、非常に安い値段にしかならないことを指す。

近義詞 捨て売り、投売り

漢 兩把東西 (指草鞋) 才值三文錢。比喻
數量多卻極為廉價，比預想的不值錢。

近 幾乎一文不值

英 As though **two bundles** of straw footwear were sold
for **only three *mons*** (obsolete smallest unit of cur-
rency in ancient Japan); Fig. To practically give something away; To sell something dirt cheap, especially for
less than something is worth.

近 sell out something for a song; a dime a dozen/two a
penny/ten a penny

224 二足の草鞋を履く _{6級}

日解與用法 一人の人間が**二足の草鞋を同時に履く**ことはできない。両立し得ない
ような二つの職業を一人ですること。江戸時代、博打打ちが博徒を取
り締まる捕吏の仕事を兼ねるような場合をいった。現在では、同時に
異なる二つの職業をこなすことをいう。

近義詞 一人二役 _{5級}

漢 穿兩雙草鞋。比喻兼任兩種完全對立
或難以兼顧的職業。源自江戶時代的
一種職業，賭徒兼捕拿盜匪的捕快。
現在單純的指一人身兼數職。

近 球員兼裁判；法官兼被告

英 **Wearing two pairs of straw sandals** at the same time;
Fig. To engage in two trades at the same time; To
take credit for doing two jobs; In the Edo period, a
gambler used to fill the role of an officer for catching
criminals.

近 wearing two hats; double in brass; get many irons in
the fires

225 日常茶飯事 _{6級}

日解與用法 日ごろお茶を飲んだり、食事をしたりすること。ごくありふれた平凡
な事柄や出来事を指す。

近義詞 ありきたりな、何の変哲もない、月並みな事柄

漢 指家中日常的茶飲飯食。比喻極其平
常的事情，司空見慣，不足為奇。

近 家常便飯

英 **A common meal, a simply homely fare**; Fig. Refers
to a routine activity that takes place everyday and is
not so significant. Nothing out of the ordinary.

近 (be) nothing to write home about; all in the day's work

226 二度あることは三度ある ⑥級

日解與用法 二度も同じことが起これば、必ずもう一度同じことが起こるということ。物事は繰り返し起こる傾向があるので、失敗や間違いを重ねないよう注意を促す時に使う言葉。普通良いことには使わない。

近義詞 歴史は繰り返す ⑥級　一災起これば二災起こる ②級

漢 有兩次就會有第三次。通常不用在正面說法，指失敗或錯誤發生兩次後必定會發生第三次。告誡人不要再犯同樣錯誤。

近 有一就有二，無三不成禮

英 **What has taken place twice will happen thrice.** Something that happens once may never happen again, but what had happened twice already is likely to happen a third time. A cliché to tell people be aware of the possible reoccurrence of failure.

近 Never twice without three times.; Bad things come in threes.; History repeats itself.

---

227 二の足を踏む ⑥級

日解與用法 一歩目は踏み出したが、**二歩目は躊躇して足踏みする**こと。決心がつかず実行をためらう、尻込みするということの喩え。

近義詞 踏ん切りが付かない ⑤級

漢 第一步踏出了但第二步原地踏步（停止腳步）。比喻因一時拿不定主意或有所顧忌，無法下定決心，畏縮不敢向前的樣子。

近 裹足不前；趑趄不前；猶豫不決；瞻前顧後

英 **To step twice in the same spot**, taking a hesitant (second) step forward; To have second thoughts before taking further action; To fail to do something through fear or lack of conviction; To shy away from doing something.

近 get cold feet; chicken out; balk at ～

---

228 二枚舌を使う ⑥級

日解與用法 まるで**舌を二枚持っているかのように使い分ける**。一つの事を二通りに言う、前後矛盾したことを言う、嘘をつく喩え。

近義詞 一口両舌 ④級　口と腹とは違う ④級

漢 用兩片舌說話，見人說人話，見鬼說鬼話。也指說話前後矛盾或指搬弄。

近 一簧兩舌；信口開河；口是心非；心口不一

英 **To use two tongues (be double-tongued)**; To tell lies or say one thing and mean something else; To say things which are contradictory; To say different things to different people about the same subject.

近 speak with a forked tongue; talk out of both sides of one's mouth

な行

229 糠に釘* 6級

日解與用法 粉状の柔らかい**米糠に釘**を打ち込むように、さっぱり手ごたえがなく、効果がないことをいう。

近義詞 暖簾に腕押し 6級　豆腐に鎹* 4級　石に灸 4級

漢 往米糠釘釘子。比喻毫無效果，徒勞無功。

近 馬尾栓豆腐

英 **To hammer a nail into rice bran**; Fig. To do something useless or futile; Be of no avail; This phrase implies that someone exerts oneself to no purpose.

近 fool's errand; like pouring water into a sieve; bolting the door with a boiled carrot

230 濡れ手で粟* 6級

日解與用法 水に**濡れた手で粟**をつかめば、たくさんの粟粒がくっついてくる。何の苦労もせずに多くの利益を得ること、骨を折らずに金を儲けることの喩え。

近義詞 一攫千金 5級　旨い汁を吸う 3級

漢 用沾濕的手抓小粟米。形容事情做起來非常容易，不花一點力氣。或比喻不用辛苦就可撈一把賺大錢，不勞而獲。

近 輕而易舉；不費吹灰之力；探囊取物

英 **To grab the millet with wet hands**; Fig. To receive the lion's share of the profit or to make big money without due effort or expense; To sit back and get what one wants.

近 easy profits; (a) get-rich-click / (to) get rich quick; make a fortune at one stroke; rake in (money)

231 猫も杓子も 6級

日解與用法 **猫も杓子**(ご飯をよそう、汁物をすくう道具)**も**、誰も彼も、どんな人も、周囲の皆が皆同じようなことをするさま。軽い軽蔑が込められるので、面と向かって使う場合は注意が必要。くだけた言い方にすれば、「どいつもこいつも」、という。女も子供もの意の「女子も弱子も」が転じた表現ともいわれる。語源は不明。

近義詞 --

漢 貓也好飯匙也罷。貓和盛飯的杓子乃至處都有，這句話含意是「不論那個人」或「那個東西」，但含有輕蔑的意思，不宜劈面對著對方說。

近 張三李四；阿貓阿狗

英 **Every cat and rice ladle** (universal to all Japanese); Fig. All ordinary individuals; all random or unknown people; Anybody or everybody; Anything or everything (Usage notes: usually said about any person or thing you do not know or even think is trivial, therefore, don't use it right to someone's face)

近 every Tom, Dick, and Harry; all the world and his wife; everybody and their dog

232 猫をかぶる ^{6級}

日解與用法 見かけは**大人しい猫のように**、本性を隠して従順そうに振る舞うことをいう。また、知っていながら知らない素振りをすることの喩え。

近義詞 かまとと、ぶりっこ

漢 戴假面具，裝成像貓一樣溫柔。意指遮掩自己的本性故作無辜狀或偽裝和善老實，或指明明知道卻裝作不知道。

近 惺惺作態；裝模作樣；佯作不知

英 **To assume oneself as a docile cat**; Fig. A person who hides his/her true colors and pretends to be friendly, innocent, ignorant or naïve; To play the hypocrite; To feign innocence.

近 (as) harmless as a kitten; (a) wolf in sheep's skin

---

233 寝た子を起こすな ^{6級}

日解與用法 ようやく**寝入った子**をわざわざ起こすな。騒ぎがせっかく収まったのに、余計なことをして問題を蒸し返すな、という。

近義詞 薮を突いて蛇を出すな ^{6級}

漢 別叫醒睡著的小孩子免得哭鬧。意指不要沒事找事，已一度了結的事情重新翻出來說。或勸人不要把好不容易平息下來的風波又蓄意挑起事端。

近 別舊事重提；別舊調重彈；別平地起風波；勿惹是生非

英 **Don't wake a sleeping baby** on purpose. Fig. Do not bring up again a problem that has been dealt with; Do not ask for trouble by rekindling an arguement which had been settled.

近 Let sleeping dogs lie.; Wake not a sleeping lion.; Don't open old wounds; Don't make a rod for your own back.

---

234 残り物には福がある ^{6級}

日解與用法 人が取り**残したもの**や最後に余ったものの中には、思いがけなく**良いもの**があるということをいう。遅れてきた人や順番が後になった人を慰める時に使われることもあれば、遠慮して何かを取り損なった人が自らを慰める言葉としても使われる。

近義詞 余り物に福がある ^{5級}　余り茶に福がある ^{3級}

漢 拿別人挑剩下的東西有福氣，最後拿的有福氣。意指剩貨中意外地也有好的東西。用來安慰名次排在後面或晚到的人只能拿些剩下的東西。也可用來自我安慰。

近 好酒沉甕底；吃鍋底有福氣

英 **It is lucky to take what is leftover.** A cliché to tell people that there is unexpected luck in what remains because people tend to save the best for last. Fig. It's last in sequence, but not last in importance. Often used when comforting people who arrive late or are low on a priority list and have to take what is left. Can be used as a thought to comfort oneself.

近 last but not least; Sometimes the lees are better than the wine.; Good luck lies in odd numbers.

な行

235 喉から手が出る 6級

日解與用法 喉の奥から手を出し、食べ物をつかみたいくらいに、欲しくてたまらないという気持ちを表す言葉。また、何が何でも手に入れたいことの喩え。

近義詞 垂涎三尺 4級

🈷 從喉嚨裡伸出手來。形容一種盼望殷切，恨不得馬上據為己有的心境。

🈲 垂涎三尺；望眼欲穿

🇬🇧 **To extend one's hand out of throat** to grab something; An idea to express someone who wants something desperately. Often used to denote a very strong desire for something that you do not have; To have a craving for possession.

🇬🇧 (would) give one's right arm for something

---

236 喉元過ぎれば熱さを忘れる* 6級

日解與用法 熱い物も飲み込んでしまえば(喉元のあたりを過ぎてしまったら)、その熱さを忘れてしまう。苦しいことも過ぎてしまえば、その時の苦しさやその時に受けた温情も簡単に忘れてしまうことの喩え。

近義詞 暑さ忘れて蔭忘る 4級　雨晴れて笠を忘る 4級　病治りて医師忘る 4級
魚を得て筌を忘る 2級

🈷 過了咽喉忘了燙。比喻事過境遷，情況好轉後立刻就忘了過去困難的時候和當時所受的恩惠。

🈲 好了傷疤忘了疼；得魚忘筌；飲水忘了掘井人

🇬🇧 **To forget the heat once it passes your throat**; Once you swallow something that's too hot, you feel relieved. The saying expresses with a degree of sarcasm that people tend to forget past hardships or gratitude when released from one's suffering.

🇬🇧 Vows made in storms are forgotten in calm.; Danger past, God forgotten.; Once on shore, we pray no more.

---

237 乗りかかった船 6級

日解與用法 船に一旦乗ってしまったら、目的地に着くまで降りたくても降りられない。ひとたび仕事に関わりを持った以上、事情が変わっても途中で止めるわけに行かないことの喩え。

近義詞 賽は投げられた 4級　騎虎の勢い 3級

🈷 一旦坐上了船。比喻已發生的事情或已進行下去的工作，即使途中有變卦，勢在必行，要停止也不允許停止，索性硬著頭皮做下去了。

🈲 騎虎難下；上了賊船；欲罷不能；一不做，二不休

🇬🇧 **Once you get on board**, you can not get off; Said when one has started something, one is unable to stop even though one wants to. One must bite the bullet and make the best of it, rather than stopping short of it. There is no way to back down.

🇬🇧 In for a penny, in for a pound. (British); In for a dime, in for a dollar. (America); have a wolf by the ears; have a tiger by the tail

238 暖簾に腕押し ⁶級

日解與用法 垂れ下がっている**暖簾を腕で押しても**、何の手ごたえもない。何の張り合いも、効果も反応もないことの喩え。

近義詞 糠に釘* ⁶級 豆腐に鎹* ⁴級

漢 用手腕去推布簾。白費力，徒勞無功。

近 水中撈月；竹籃打水；勞而無功

英 **To push one's arms against the hanging curtain** (in the doorway of a shop or a house); Making an useless and completely ineffective effort; Making futile attempts; To take an action which elicits no response, like pouring water into a sieve.

近 beat the air/wind; bite on granite

239 掃き溜めに鶴 ⁶級

日解與用法 汚いごみ捨て場に現れたひときわ美しい鶴。つまらないものの中に飛び抜けて優れたものが現れることの喩え。「掃き溜め」に喩えられる側にとっては極めて不愉快な表現であるので、使用に注意が必要。

近義詞 鶏群の一鶴 ⁴級

漢 垃圾堆裏出現的鶴。比喻一個人的才能在周圍一群人裏顯得很突出，與眾不同，亦比喻拙劣的群體中出現非常優秀的人材。對被形容為「垃圾堆裏」的人而言，是一句非常不友善不愉快的話，因此宜看場合使用。

近 鶴立難群；出類拔萃

英 **Like a crane in a dump**, a jewel in a dunghill; Said about someone who is is considered somewhat out of place and is distinguished from one's kind (Usage notes: usually the saying may offend people who are around the person you praised, therefore, be careful when you use it). The bee's knees; The cat's whiskers.

近 triton among the minnows

240 薄氷を踏む ⁶級

日解與用法 今にも割れそうな**薄く張った氷の上を**ひやひやしながら**歩く**。極めて危険な状態に臨むことの喩え。中国の古典に由来する表現。

近義詞 虎の尾を踏む ³級 累卵の危うき ³級

漢 像踩在薄冰上一樣。比喻面臨極為危險的情況，使人存有戒心。

近 （如臨深淵）如履薄冰；提心吊膽；春冰虎尾；危如累卵

英 **Like walking on thin ice** (borrowed from a Chinese proverb); Fig. To be in a very precarious and risky position, on the image of someone walking on something that offers little support and may collapse at any moment.

近 walk on thin ice/skate on thin ice; walk on eggs/eggshells

241 箸にも棒にも掛からない 6級

日解與用法 細い**箸**にも、太い**棒**にも引っ掛からない。あまりにもひどすぎて、取り扱いに困り、どうにもこうにも手がつけられないこと。また、何の取り柄もなく、使い物にならないこと。

近義詞 縄にも葛にもかからない 3級 酢でも蒟蒻でも 3級

漢 用細筷子也好用粗棒子也好都夾不起來。意指差勁到拿他沒辦法的人或事物。或指一無可取之處的人或事物。

近 不可救藥；一無是處；衣架飯囊；文不成童生，武不成鐵兵

英 Can't pick up by thin chopsticks or even thick sticks. Said about a person or thing that is too bad to be applied to almost every aspect. Be devoid of anything useful. Can be used as a rebuke, implying that the person or thing you are addressing lacks even a single redeeming feature. Someone who is "hopeless".

近 (be) past praying for; Past cure, past care. ; (a) dead duck

242 蜂の巣をつついたよう 6級

日解與用法 **蜂の巣をつつく**と、蜂が次から次へと巣から飛び出すように、大騒ぎとなって手に負えない、収拾がつかないさま。

近義詞 てんやわんや

漢 好像戳了蜂巢一樣，蜜蜂四處逃竄。比喻掀起了一陣大騷動，無法收拾。

近 捅馬蜂窩

英 Like poking a honeycomb; Fig. A state of uproar or confusion, like a madhouse; To create a lot of trouble; To lead to turmoil; To be thrown into a total chaos.

近 stir up a hornet's nest; make the fur fly

243 八方美人 6級

日解與用法 どこから見ても欠点のない美人の意から、誰にも悪く思われないように、如才なく振る舞う人。悪い意味で用いられることが多い。

近義詞 八面玲瓏 3級

漢 八面(完美無缺的)美人。比喻一個人待人接物面面俱到，處世圓融。一般多用於貶義，指人非常世故，想討好所有的人。

近 八面見光；八面玲瓏；刀切豆腐兩面光

英 An all-around (eight-sided) beauty; Fig. Someone who is able to easily blend into any social situation in a smart way or who charms and flatters everyone seeming to be their friend (it usually has a negative connotation).

近 All things to all men.; (be) everybody's friend

は行

244 鳩が豆鉄砲を食ったよう [6級]

日解與用法 鳩が豆鉄砲（大豆を弾き飛ばす竹製の玩具）で撃たれ、何があったんだろと、驚いて目を丸くしている様子。思いがけない出来事に驚いて、きょとんとしていることの喩え。

近義詞 気が動転する

漢 像鴿子被豆子砲射到一樣。比喻事出突然，猝不及防，眼睛發直發愣，驚慌地不知所措的樣子。

近 驚慌失措；雞飛狗跳；六神無主

英 **Like a pigeon who's been shot by a peashooter** (a toy gun loaded with beans). Fig. Something stuns you out of your wits. Said about someone who is wearing a stupid look of surprise. A mental state of emotional arousal caused by fear or panic that makes you look dumbfounded.

近 like a duck in a thunderstorm; like a deer caught in the headlights

245 早起きは三文の得 [6級]

日解與用法 朝早く起きれば、三文の銭を儲けることができる。わずか三文の利益だとしても、何かしら良いことがあるという。早起きを奨励する意味を込めて使う言葉。健康にも良いし、仕事や勉強もはかどる、ということ。

近義詞 早起き千両 [3級]　宵寝朝起き長者の基 [3級]

漢 早起能掙得三文錢，三文錢雖然很少，但此句話乃鼓勵人早起。起得早不但有益身心，頭腦清醒，精力充沛，對工作或唸書也都有助益。

近 早起的鳥兒有蟲吃；早起三光，晚起三慌

英 **One who wakes early gains three** *mon* (small coin). An expression indicating that if you keep early hours, you may always be healthier, it's good for studying and working too.

近 The early bird catches the worm.; Early to bed and early to rise, makes a man healthy, wealthy, and wise. (Benjamin Franklin); He that would thrive must rise at five.

246 腹が減っては戦が出来ぬ [6級]

日解與用法 腹が空いていたのでは十分に活動ができない、もちろん戦うことはできない。いい働きをしようと思ったら、まず腹ごしらえをしろという教え。

近義詞 兵隊は腹で動く [3級]

漢 飢兵瘦馬不能打仗，空腹者無法從事任何活動，更不用說打仗了。強調填飽肚皮才能幹活，沒吃飽什麼事也做不了的。

近 皇家不差餓兵；兵馬未動，糧草先行；民以食為天；人是鐵，飯是鋼，一頓不吃餓得慌

英 **You can't fight on an empty stomach.** Fig. It is hard to labor with an empty belly, let alone fight in a battle; People need a supply of food in order to keep on fighting; Bread is the staff of life.

近 The stomach carries the feet.; An army marches on its stomach. (Napoleon)

247 腹八分に医者いらず _{6級}

日解與用法 **腹に八分目程度食べていれば病気にかかることはない。**お腹いっぱい食べるより、軽めの食事の方が身体を健康に保つということ。暴飲暴食を戒めていう言葉。

近義詞 腹も身の内 _{4級}

漢 飯吃八分飽不用看醫生。比喻克制飲食比飽餐一頓健康。勸人飲食要節制。

近 少吃嘗滋味，多吃傷脾胃；夜飯少吃口，活到九十九

英 **To keep your belly eight-tenths full will keep the doctor away**; Fig. Suggesting that moderation and self-restraint from food will keep you healthy, in contrast, always stuffing oneself with food may make one less healthy.

近 Temperance is the best physic.; Feed by measure and defy the physician.; Gluttony kills more than the sword. (George Herbert)

248 必要は発明の母 _{6級}

日解與用法 発明は必要に迫られて生まれるものだということ。必要に迫られると、あれこれ工夫がなされ発明を生むから、**必要は発明にとって母親のようなもの**だということ。英語のことわざの訳語。

近義詞 窮すれば通ず _{4級}

漢 需要是發明之母。需要啓發創造，因此說需要是發明的母親、原動力。此日本的諺語和中文一樣乃源自英文成語。

近 需要是發明之母

英 **Necessity is the mother of invention** (a direct translation from English). Fig. When people really need something, they will figure out a way to do it. Most inventions are created to solve some problems.

近 Necessity is the mother of invention.

249 一筋縄では行かぬ _{6級}

日解與用法 **一本の縄（転じて、普通の方法や手段）では対処できないということ。**ありきたりの、当たり前のやり方では、簡単にはうまくいかないことを指す。また、手ごわい相手の意味を指すこともある。

近義詞 煮ても焼いても食えぬ _{4級}

漢 一條普通的繩子無法擺平。意即只用普通的辦法行事行不通，例如一個棘手或令人尷尬的問題無法用平淡無奇的方法去應付。也比喻一個「難搞」的人或事。

近 棘手難事；軟硬不吃的人

英 **Can't be dealt with by ordinary "ropes (means)"**; Said to describe an deep-rooted issue which defies any conventional attempt at solving. It's no easy matter dealing with a hassle or a tough cookie.

近 (a) tough/hard nut to crack

は行

250 人の噂も七十五日 ^{6級}

日解與用法 世間での噂や評判は長く続くものではなく、**七十五日も経てば**自然に**忘れ去られてしまう**ものだということ。どんな噂が立ってもそれは一時的なものに過ぎず、放っておけば良いという意味が込められている。

近義詞 世の取り沙汰も七十五日 ^{3級}　良きも悪しきも七十五日 ^{3級}

漢 別人的閒話最多傳個七十五天。比喻流言蜚語或街談巷議日子一久就不新鮮了，不久即被淡忘掉的。意指不必去理會那些愛說長道短的人。

近 謠言止於智者

英 **Gossip lasts just 75 days.** A saying to tell people that, do not get too upset about gossip, as it attracts much attention just for a while but is soon forgotten; Don't let a little rumor bother you as people have short memories.

近 A wonder lasts but nine days.

251 人の口に戸は立てられぬ ^{6級}

日解與用法 人の口の戸を閉めることは出来ない。世間の噂は、防ごうとしても防げない、噂の種とならないように気をつけなさい、という教え。

近義詞 開いた口には戸は立てぬ ^{5級}　口から出れば世間 ^{3級}

漢 人嘴難封。比喻人言可畏，謠言總會被傳來傳去，暗示人們不要落人話柄。

近 (瓶嘴扎得住) 人嘴扎不住；嘴長在人家臉上

英 **You cannot fix doors on people's mouths.** Fig. You cannot hold people's tongues. Once people get started gossiping, it's hard to stop them. Don't fall victim to the watercooler gossip.

近 Anyone can start a rumor, but none can stop one.

252 人の褌で相撲を取る ^{6級}

日解與用法 他人の褌を借りて相撲を取る。他人のものをちゃっかり利用して、抜け目なく自分の利益を計ったり、自分の役目を果たしたりすることの喩え。

近義詞 人の牛蒡で法事する ^{4級}　人の提灯で明かり取る ^{4級}　他人の念仏で極楽参り ^{4級}

漢 用別人的丁字褲玩摔跤。巧借他人之物成己之事或為自己謀利。譴責或暗指一個卑鄙的人用盡心機作利己之事。

近 借花獻佛

英 **To take part in a wrestling match by wearing a borrowed** *sumo* **loincloth** (a *sumo* wrestler's *mawasi*, an ornamental apron). Fig. Said as a rebuke, implying that the person you are addressing is unfairly reaping the benefits or being generous at someone else's expense; somewhat cheeky and calculating behavior.

近 Always draw the snake from its hole with another man's hand.

は行

253 人を見たら泥棒と思え [6級]

日解與用法 他人を見たら、うかつに信用しないで、まずは**相手が泥棒だと**疑ってかかるくらい、用心しろということ。

近義詞 人を見たら鬼と思え [3級]　火を見たら火事と思え [3級]

漢 看到不熟的人就把他當賊防。意指不可輕信別人，對任何陌生人持懷疑的眼光，留神觀察。

近 防人之心不可無；逢人只說三分話，不可全拋一片心

英 **When you meet a stranger, regard him/her as a thief.** (try to examine anyone you meet who he/she is) ; Fig. A cliché to tell people you should not be too ready to trust a stranger. You can never be too careful, call everything into question. To take heed and keep on the alert against any stranger.

近 Trust is the mother of deceit.; They that think none ill are soonest beguiled.; take (someone's words) with a grain of salt; Let the buyer beware.

254 火に油を注ぐ [6級]

日解與用法 燃えている**火に油を注ぐ**と、ますます火勢が強まる。勢いの激しいものがいっそう勢いを増すことの喩えで、事態がいっそう悪化してしまう望ましくない行為を指す。

近義詞 薪に油を添える [4級]　駆け馬に鞭 [3級]

漢 在燃燒的火頭上加上油。比喻助長事態的發展，使情況變得比原來更加惡化。

近 火上加油；變本加厲

英 **To pour fuel on the fire**, causing a flame to grow larger; Fig. To do something that makes a bad situation worse; To make an angry person get even angrier; To make something more intense.

近 add fuel to the fire/flame; fan the flames (of something)

255 火の無い所に煙は立たぬ [6級]

日解與用法 全く**火の気がない所**から**煙は立たない**。うわさが立つのは、何かしらその根拠なり理由なりがあるからに違いない、という喩え。英語圏の言い回しの訳語。

近義詞 煙あれば火あり [4級]

漢 沒有火的地方不會冒煙。意指事情發生，總有個原因。謠言不可能無緣無故的冒出來，即使無中生有也必定有其理由。

近 無風不起浪

英 **Smoke doesn't rise in places with no fire.** Means that when people cast doubt about something, there is a good reason for the suspicion, there is usually some truth behind every rumor. When there is evidence of a problem, there probably is a problem as well.

近 (There's) no smoke without fire.; Where there's smoke there's fire.

は行

95

256 ピンからキリまで ^{6級}

日解與用法 「ピン」は「一」、「初め、最高」。「キリ」は「十」、「終わり、最低」という意味から、文脈によって ①最上のものから最低のものまで ②最初から最後まで ③様々、いろいろ、という意味合いで使われる。

近義詞 ぴんきり

漢 應有盡有，指從最高等級到最低等級，從頭到尾的各種等級類別。

近 三六九等

英 **From first to last; From start to finish; From the best to the worst**, which cover a wide range to choose from, which come in all qualities and grades; A cliché to imply all sort of things.

近 run the gamut from the best to the worst; from soup to nuts

---

257 風前の灯火 ^{6級}

日解與用法 風の当たるところにある灯火は、今にも消えそうになる。物事が危険にさらされていて、非常に危ない情況をいう。人の命に対してもいう。

近義詞 風前の灯燭の如し ^{4級}

漢 像被風吹的燭火一樣快要熄滅。形容危險迫在眼前，亦比喻人生命垂危，奄奄一息或到了接近死亡的晚年。

近 風前殘燭；風燭殘年；行將就木；危在旦夕；岌岌可危；命若懸絲

英 **Like a candlelight flickering in the wind**; An expression used to describe a precarious and unstable situation, or imply an elderly person who have one foot in the grave.

近 His candle burns within the socket.; within an inch of one's life; on the verge of life and death; (something) hang by a thread

---

258 下手な鉄砲も数撃ちゃ当たる ^{6級}

日解與用法 射撃が下手でも、数多く撃っているうちにまぐれで一発ぐらいは命中することはあるという意。試みる回数が多ければ多いほど成功の数も多くなる、ということ。目上の人などに直接言うと失礼な場合もあるので注意が必要。

近義詞 下手な鍛冶屋も一度は名剣 ^{3級}

漢 槍法再不好多打幾次也能命中。意指多試幾次勝算必也提高。含貶意，不宜對長輩用。

近 亂槍打鳥，不中也難

英 **Even an unskilled gunner will hit the target by sheer luck if he tried enough.** Fig. An implication said that a large number of attempts will lead to a higher odds of success (avoid using this phrase with your elders and betters because it sounds offensive).

近 He that shoots oft, at last shall hit the mark.

は行

96

259 蛇に見込まれた蛙 6級

日解與用法 恐ろしいものや苦手なものを前にして、身がすくんで動けなくなることの喩え。**蛙は蛇に睨まれる**と、恐ろしさのあまりちぢこまってしまうことをいう。

近義詞 蛇に睨まれた蛙 4級　鷹の前の雀 4級　猫の前の鼠 4級

漢 像被蛇盯住的青蛙一樣，形容極度驚嚇，恐懼萬分。

近 魂不附體；魂飛魄散；提心吊膽

英 **Like a frog being stared down by a snake**; Fig. Being stunned or paralyzed with fear which makes you unable to move or think. Be scared out of one's wits.

近 like Daniel in the lions' den; (be) in a blue funk; like a deer caught in the headlights

260 ペンは剣よりも強し 6級

日解與用法 **剣よりもペンは強い。**言論の力は武力よりも人々の心に訴える力を持っている。文章で表現される思想は世論を動かし、武力以上に強い影響力を持っていることの喩え。英語圏の言い回しの訳語。

近義詞 文は武にまさる 4級

漢 筆墨勝於刀劍。拿筆桿子的人比拿槍桿子的人更厲害。意指言論思想的力量遠勝於軍事武力，影響人心輿論。源自英文的格言。

近 文勝於武

英 **The pen is mightier than the sword** (a direct translation from English saying). Fig. Said to emphasize that thinking and writing have more influence on people than the use of force or violence.

近 The pen is mightier than the sword.

261 墓穴を掘る 6級

口解與用法 自分を葬るための**墓の穴を**自分の手で**掘る。**自分から進んで身を滅ぼす原因を作ってしまうことの喩え。

近義詞 破滅の一途を辿る 4級

漢 自己的所作所為就像替自己挖掘墳墓一樣。比喻自尋死路。

近 自掘墳墓；玩火自焚

英 **To dig a hole/grave for oneself**; Fig. To get oneself into a difficult situation; to bring calamity upon oneself ; Be responsible for one's own downfall; To do something stupid that will cause problems for oneself; To face the problem of one's own making.

近 dig oneself into a hole/dig one's own grave; shoot oneself in the foot; hoist with/by one's own petard; If you play with fire, you get burned.

は行

97

262 仏造って魂入れず 6級

日解與用法 仏像を造っても目を描き入れなかったため、**魂が宿らない**こと。苦心して作ってきた物の仕上げの段階で、肝心要な点を抜かすことの喩え。また、最も重要な一事を欠いたために何の役にも立たなくなることをいう。

近義詞 画竜点睛を欠く 5級

漢 造了佛像卻未點眼睛，未賦予靈氣。形容少了最重要的關鍵，因而事情等於白做，很可惜。

近 畫龍未點睛；功虧一簣

英 **Making Buddhist statue without adding the soul in it.** This is known during a consecration ceremony held in Japan to animate a new statue by painting its eyes. With the statue just short of its eyes, all that could have been achieved is unfortunately spoiled. It implies that someone failed to bring a work of art to life due to the lack of a final significant effort.

近 lack the finishing touch; within an ace of doing something

263 蒔かぬ種は生えぬ* 6級

日解與用法 種を蒔かなければ芽が出ず、花も実もなるはずがない。原因がなければ結果は生じない。努力もせずに良い成果を期待するのは無理だという教え。

近義詞 打たぬ鐘は鳴らぬ 3級　春植えざれば秋実らず 3級

漢 籽不種不長，也不會開花結實。形容不努力就別指望有好的結果，不勞則無穫。或比喻事出必有因，沒因即無果。

近 一分耕耘，一分收穫；種瓜得瓜，種豆得豆；春不種，秋不收；鼓不打不響，鐘不撞不鳴

英 **Unsown seeds will not sprout.** Everything that happens to you is a result of your own actions, you only get out what you put in, so you must work hard to achieve things.

近 You reap what you sow./As you sow, so shall you reap.; He who sows a little, shall reap little; he who sows much will reap much.; Nothing will come of nothing.; No mill, no meal.

264 俎板の鯉 6級

日解與用法 まな板に乗せられた鯉が、ただ調理されるのを待っている状態の意。逃げ場のない者がなす術もなく相手の意のままになる、相手に生殺与奪の権を握られている状態にあることをいう。中国の成語に由来。

近義詞 生簀の鯉 3級　俎上の魚 3級

漢 像菜刀板上的鯉魚。比喻自己受制於人，處在任人宰割受人擺布的境遇。意指生殺大權掌握在別人手中。

近 人為刀俎，我為魚肉；魚游釜中

英 **A carp on the chopping board** (taken from a Chinese saying); Fig. Used when one feels like a ship at the mercy of the storm, is not free to behave in the way that they would like. In the clutches of someone who holds an authority of their life over them; The destiny of someone has been determined.

近 someone's fate is sealed; someone's hands are tied

265 眉に唾をつける ⑥級

日解與用法 **眉に唾をつければ**狐や狸に化かされないという俗信がある。うまい話に乗らない、いかがわしい人物に騙されないように眉に唾をつけて用心する。真偽の疑わしいものを略して「眉唾物」、「眉唾」という。

近義詞 --

漢 在眉毛上抹唾液（日本古時相傳抹唾液在眉毛上，就可提防狐狸精欺騙）。形容保持警覺，時刻警惕。「眉唾物」指不可輕信的人或物。

近 提防上當；提防小人

英 **If you wet your eyebrows with saliva, the fox will not bewitch you** (one old superstitious well-known behavior in ancient Japan) Fig. Be wary of something dubious; Be on one's guard against fake or trickery by examining it very carefully.

近 Keep your wits about you.; take (something) with a grain of salt

266 真綿で首を絞めるよう ⑥級

日解與用法 真綿は柔らかいが、引っ張っても千切れないくらい強い。その**真綿で首を絞めれば**、じりじりと首に食い込んでいく。じわじわと、遠まわしに人を責めたり、痛めつけたりすることの喩え。

近義詞 真綿で喉を絞める ④級

漢 用絲綿掐脖子。絲綿柔軟結實，最先不感到疼痛，日久則疼痛難忍。比喻使人在不知不覺中受到折磨。慢慢地以刻薄的詞句打擊一個人，使其不得安寧。

近 軟刀子殺人

英 **To strangle a person's neck with silk floss.** Said about a way of having a strong argument but delivering it in a very gentle way. Attacking or admonishing people with words imperceptibly and slowly; Wearing someone down by constant nagging.

近 Use soft words and hard arguments.

267 ミイラ取りがミイラになる ⑥級

日解與用法 防腐剤に使う**ミイラ油を取りに出かけた者がミイラになってしまう。**人を連れ戻しに行った者が、先方にとどまって役目を果たさないことをいう。また、相手を説得しようとした者が、逆に相手に説得されてしまう意。

近義詞 木兎引きが木兎に引かれる ③級

漢 去拿木乃伊防腐用油的人自己成了木乃伊。形容打算去叫別人回來結果自己一去不返。或形容本想去說服別人結果反而被對方說服。

近 適得其反；弄巧成拙；肉包子打狗，有去無回

英 **The person who seeks a preservative oil for making a mummy becomes a mummy himself.** The hunter becomes the hunted. Fig. To try to bring someone home for some purpose but end up with the opposite result than intended; To try to convince someone only to end up being convinced instead.

近 Go for wool and come home shorn.; The biter bit.

268 見ざる聞かざる言わざる 6級

日解與用法 心を惑わすものについて、**見ない、聞かない、話さない**。打ち消しの文語助動詞「ず」の連体形「ざる」を「猿」にかけて、両目、両耳、口それぞれを両手で覆った三匹の猿の像、「見猿聞か猿言わ猿」を「三猿」という。

近義詞 --

漢 不看、不聽、不說那些使人困惑，無益身心的東西。日本自古以三隻猴子遮住眼睛，耳朵和嘴巴來表達。（取「ざる」之諧音唸成「猿」→猴子）

近 非禮勿視，非禮勿聽，非禮勿言

英 **Don't see, don't hear, don't speak** what is not good for your body and soul. To ignore any evil that bewilders you or comes in contact with you (often represented by three monkeys at various shrines, sitting side by side, one of which is covering its eyes, the next its ears, and the third its mouth).

近 See no evil, hear no evil, speak no evil.

269 三日坊主 6級

日解與用法 **短期間 (三日) の坊主修行**。せっかく出家しても、戒律の厳しさに堪えかねてすぐに還俗してしまう僧がいることから出来た言葉。飽きやすく、何をしても長続きしないこと。また、そのような人。

近義詞 蛇稽古 3級　一暴十寒 3級

漢 僅當三天和尚。指對學習或工作沒定性，沒有恆心，不能長期堅持的人。

近 三天打魚，兩天曬網；一曝十寒

英 **A priest/monk for three days**; Fig. A disparaging remark about any capricious person who quickly shows enthusiasm for anything but cannot stick to it, soon giving up.

近 do something by/in fits and starts

270 耳に胼胝が出来る 6級

日解與用法 **耳に角質化した厚い皮膚 (胼胝) ができる**ほど、同じ話を何度も繰り返し聞かされて、うんざりするさまを表す言葉。

近義詞 口を酸っぱくして言う 5級

漢 喋喋不休，相同的話聽了千遍萬遍，**聽得耳朵都要長繭了**。形容老調重彈，一直嘮叨個沒完沒了，講到讓聽的人煩膩的受不了。胼胝乃皮膚長期受壓磨擦後表層變厚變硬的現象。

近 耳朵生繭；聽不完兜著走

英 To be told something thousands of times that you **get calluses on your ears** (get fed up with hearing the same topic); To emphasize when you're sick of listening to someone's constant talking. In other words, when someone harps on the same string far more than is appreciated, it irritates you.

近 talk someone's ear off

271 虫が知らせる ⑥級

<ruby>虫<rt>むし</rt></ruby>が<ruby>知<rt>し</rt></ruby>らせる

日解與用法 **虫の知らせ。**何かが起こりそうな予感がして胸騒ぎがする意。古く、中国の道教では、「三尸九虫」という虫が体内にいて、心の中の意識や感情を呼び起こしたり、色々な病気を引き起こしたりすると考えられていた。理由が分からなく、説明のできない事柄を "虫のせい" にしたという。

近義詞 第六感 ⑥級

漢 **蟲的提示**、意指不祥的預感。古代中國的道教謂人體內部棲有三屍九蟲，喚起人的意識、感覺、感情或引發病症。對於無法理解或控制的狀況，往往就推說是這些「蟲」在搗亂作祟。

近 不祥之兆

英 **Clue from a worm**; Fig. To have a vague foreboding, an uneasy premonition; In ancient China, people believed that there were nine worms which live in the human body, arousing feeling and thought in the deep in mind or causing a disorder of body.

近 (one's) gut feeling tells …; feel something in one's bones

272 虫の居所が悪い ⑥級

<ruby>虫<rt>むし</rt></ruby>の<ruby>居所<rt>いどころ</rt></ruby>が<ruby>悪<rt>わる</rt></ruby>い

日解與用法 体内に棲みついているといわれる**虫が居心地が悪い**と感じた時、人間が怒りっぽくなる。機嫌が悪い様子を言い表す。普段は気にしないような些細なことでも気に障り、人に当たり散らすのは、体の中にいる虫によるものだと考えられている。（271 句の説明を参照）

近義詞 臍を曲げる ⑤級　ご機嫌斜め ⑥級

漢 比喻火氣大舉止反常是因為人體內的**蟲子在作怪**、處處覺得不對勁。對平常根本不在乎的一點兒芝麻小事就大發雷霆。請查閱第 271 句說明。

近 吃錯藥

英 **The worm is in a bad spot.** Said about someone who gets in a bad mood and is easily annoyed for no particular reason. See previous quote #271 for more information.

近 get out of bed on the wrong side/wake up on the wrong side of the bed; (be) like a bear with a sore head

273 目糞鼻糞を笑う ⑥級

<ruby>目糞<rt>めくそ</rt></ruby><ruby>鼻糞<rt>はなくそ</rt></ruby>を<ruby>笑<rt>わら</rt></ruby>う

日解與用法 **汚い目やにが、鼻糞を「汚い」とあざ笑う**意。自分の欠点には気がつかないで、他人の似たような欠点を笑うことの喩え。また、笑う者も、笑われる者も大した違いはないということの喩え。

近義詞 五十歩百歩 ⑥級　猿の尻笑い ④級

漢 眼垢笑鼻屎髒。比喻只知嘲笑別人缺點卻未想到自己亦半斤八兩。

近 五十步笑百步；烏鴉笑豬黑，龜笑鱉無尾；禿子笑和尚

英 **Eye discharge is laughing at nose snot.** Fig. It makes no difference to the accuser if he or she has the same fault as the person he is accusing.

近 The pot calling the kettle black.; The chimney-sweeper bids the collier wash his face.

274 目には目を歯には歯を ^{6級}

日解與用法 目を傷つけられたら相手の目を傷つけ、歯を折られたら相手の歯を折る。害を受けたら、それに相応する報復をすることの意。他人から受けた危害や損害に対して同等の仕返しをする古代の処罰法（タリオ）。ハンムラビ法典、旧約聖書出エジプト記に「目には目」という記述がある。

近義詞 血で血を洗う ^{5級}

漢 如果被毀掉眼睛則毀掉對方的眼睛，若被折斷牙齒則折斷對方的牙齒。指對方使用什麼手段，就用什麼手段進行回擊。是一種古代法律制裁的概念。漢模拉比法典與舊約聖經裡的出埃及記裏有此一節表述。

近 以牙還牙，以眼還眼；以血濯血

英 **An eye for an eye and a tooth for a tooth.** Used to refer to the belief that a person who treats others badly should be treated in the same way; The notion that for every wrong done, there should be a compensating measure of justice, as an old law of Talion. The passage was also shown in the Code of Hammurabi and Old Testament, Oxodus.

近 An eye for an eye and a tooth for a tooth.; Blood will have blood.; tit for tat; measure for measure

275 目の上の瘤* ^{6級}

日解與用法 目のすぐ上にたんこぶが出来ると、始終気になってうっとうしい。自分よりも地位や能力が上で、何かにつけて目障りで邪魔になるものをいう。

近義詞 目の上のたんこぶ ^{6級}　鼻の先の疣々 ^{4級}

漢 眼睛上面的疔瘡。比喻一個看不順眼，心目中最痛恨、最討厭的人（通常針對地位或能力比自己強的人）

近 眼中釘，肉中刺；心頭之患

英 **A swelling over the eyes**; Fig. An eyesore to you, a person that repeatedly annoys you or causes you pain, ususally indicates someone who has a higher position or is superior to you.

近 (a) thorn in someone's side/(a) thorn in the flesh; (a) pain in the neck/butt; pet peeve

276 目の中に入れても痛くない ^{6級}

日解與用法 目の中に入れても痛みを感じないほど、子や孫が可愛くて可愛くて堪らない、見境なく可愛がるさまをいう。

近義詞 虎の子のように大事にする ^{5級}

漢 就算放到眼睛裏也不會痛。強調溺愛兒孫的程度，百般呵護，疼到骨子裡。拿在手裏怕跌著，含在嘴裏怕化了，頂在頭上怕嚇了。

近 心肝寶貝；掌上明珠

英 **It wouldn't hurt even putting one's kids into one's eyes.** Fig. Doting on one's kids or grandkids all the more; Refers to someone who loves their kids or grandkids more than anything in the world and spoils them.

近 (the) apple of one's eye

ま行

102

277 目は口ほどに物を言う ⑥級

日解與用法 感情のこもった**眼差しは口で話すのと同じくらい**、相手の心を捉え、相手に**気持ちを伝える**ことができるということ。喜怒哀楽の情はまず目に表れる。

近義詞 目が物をいう ④級　目は心の鏡 ④級

漢 眼睛像嘴巴一樣會說話，眼能傳神而流露內心的想法。意指所有喜怒哀樂都會體現在眼神，和語言一樣能傳情達意。

近 眉目傳情；眼睛為心靈之窗

英 **The eyes speak as much as the mouth**, eyes could best express the emotion and convey the message in your mind. Fig. A person's thoughts can be ascertained by looking in his/her eyes; Eyes are as eloquent as the tongue; Love needs no words.

近 The eyes are the window to the soul.; The eyes have one language everywhere.; The heart's letter is read in the eyes.

278 目を丸くする ⑥級

日解與用法 **驚いて目を大きく（丸く）見開く**。驚愕のあまり、目を見張る。びっくりした時の表情をいう。

近義詞 生き肝を抜く ⑤級　ど肝を抜く ⑤級　舌を巻く ⑤級

漢 圓睜著眼的樣子。聽到一些驚訝的事情或是難以置信令人傻眼的事實時，所浮現出的一種神情。

近 目瞪口呆

英 **Be round-eyed** with amazement; Be astonished **with wide-open eyes**; Fig. If people have their eyes opened very wide, they are likely very surprised or in disbelief.

近 stare in wonder

279 持ちつ持たれつ ⑥級

日解與用法 **お互いに支え合って、助けたり助けられたりする**さま。並立助詞の「～つ～つ」は対照的な動作が交互に行われることを示す。または、複数の事柄を並列する「～たり～たり」の意で使われることもある。

近義詞 お互い様

漢 扶持他人也被他人扶持。意指互相依靠，互相幫助。「～つ～つ」於日文語法中謂之「並立助詞」，是指兩個對等的行動交互進行，例如浮きつ沈みつ（乍浮乍沈）。或指並列的兩個動作，例如追いつ追われつ（你追我趕）。

近 禮尚往來

英 **To support and to be supported** (to support each other); To give and to take; Fig. Cooperation benefits us all 「～つ～つ form」means 「～たり～たり」, it is followed by how or why those actions occurred, the two verbs can be either contradictory actions or reciprocal actions.

近 One hand washes the other.; You scratch my back, and I'll scratch yours.; No man is an island.

ま行

280 元も子もない ^{6級}

日解與用法 **元金も利子もない。**投資して利益を得るどころか元手までなくしてしまうこと。欲張りすぎて無理した結果、失敗してすべてを失うことの喩え。金銭的なことだけではなく、今までの努力が何もかも無駄になることの喩えにも用いられる。「元も子も失う」ともいう。

近義詞 すっからかん

漢 本利盡失。意指徹底的失敗導致全盤虧損，一無所有。

近 難飛蛋打；賠了夫人又折兵

英 **Having lost both the interest and the principal;** Fig. Used when someone emphasized that one has lost all of one's assets.

近 dead loss; lose one's shirt off one's back

281 もぬけの殻 ^{6級}

日解與用法 「蛻」は**蛇や蝉が脱皮すること**、また、**脱皮した後の皮**の意。その抜け殻の中が空っぽであることから、①人が逃げ去ったあとの寝床や住居を指す ②魂が抜けた身体、気力や生気のないさまをいう。

近義詞 セミの抜け殻

漢 蛇或蟬脱皮後剩下的外皮。①意指犯人脱身逃走後人去樓空的房子。②也可比喻一個徒具形骸毫無生氣的人。

近 ①金蟬脱殼 ②行屍走肉

英 **Skin cast off the snake or cicada;** Fig. ① A completely empty, uninhabited house where a criminal have fled. ② A person who loses his or her vigor.

近 ① a desert hideout ② walk like a zombie; (a) walking dead/corpse

282 桃栗三年柿八年* ^{6級}

日解與用法 芽が出て実がなるまでに、**桃と栗は三年、柿は八年**かかるということ。何事も成し遂げるまでには相応の年月が必要だという喩え。結果を急ぐことを戒める言葉として使うことが多い。

近義詞 首振り三年ころ八年 ^{3級}

漢 發芽後，三年結桃和栗，八年結柿。意指任何事情都要有一段時間才能收成，急也急不得。這句話告誡人們「別著急」！

近 十年樹木（百年樹人）；瓜熟蒂落

英 **Planted peach and chestnut seeds take three years to bear fruit, persimmons take eight.** Said that it often bears the fruit of one's actions in a reasonable length of time; Be patient!

近 Everything comes in its own good time.; Hold your horses!; Walnuts and pears you plant for your heirs.

283 藪から棒* 6級

日解與用法 **不意に藪から棒が突き出る。** 出し抜けに物事が行われることの喩え。また、何の前触れや前置きもなく予期せぬ出来事に遭遇した様子を表す。

近義詞 青天の霹靂 6級　寝耳に水* 6級

漢 草叢中突然捅出一根棒子。意指做出讓人感覺唐突冒昧的舉動。或指事出突然，發生出乎意料的事。

近 突如其來；晴天霹靂

英 **A cudgel from a bamboo thicket.** Fig. To carry out something all of a sudden without any previous notice; To refer to something that you do not expect to happen.

近 a bolt from the blue; Scarborough Warning

284 藪を突いて蛇を出す 6級

日解與用法 **藪を突いてわざわざ蛇を追い出す。** 収まっていることに余計な手出しをして、思いもしない悪い結果を招くことの喩え。略して「やぶ蛇」。中国語の成句「打草驚蛇」の意味と異なる。

近義詞 寝た子を起こす 6級　草を打って蛇を驚かす 4級

漢 從草叢中故意趕蛇出來。比喻無緣無故找盆子，把一度了結的事情重新搬出來說，蓄意挑起事端。（與中文的「打草驚蛇」意思不同）

近 無事生非；自找麻煩；咎由自取

英 **To scare out a snake by poking at a bamboo thicket**; Fig. To create a situation that will cause trouble for oneself. To make the fur fly by bringing up an issue that has already been concluded. This is often wrongly confused with the Chinese idiom「打草驚蛇」which takes on a different meaning though it literally looks similar.

近 beat a dead horse; open a can of worms; Let well enough alone.

285 病は気から 6級

日解與用法 **病気は気の持ち方一つで、** 病状が重くもなれば軽くもなるという。気をしっかり持ちな、と病人を励ます時に使われる。しかし、そのメカニズムに関しては科学的根拠が得られておらず、その考え方について温度差があるため、使う相手に配慮が必要。

近義詞 百病は気から起こる 3級　病気は気で勝つ 3級

漢 病打心情起，心境情緒有時會影響病情，可能轉好亦可能轉壞。因個人情況而異，若用來關懷病人，須留意用法。

近 積鬱成疾

英 **Getting sick from concern**; Fig. Willpower can influence disease. It is believed that one's mind rules the body, being positive will take a change for the better, and vice versa, but it depends. The patient may be not freed from illness just by this saying, however.

近 (Mindset may) kill or cure.; Care killed the cat.

や行

286 羊頭狗肉 ^{6級}

日解與用法 看板に偽りあり。**羊の頭を看板に掲げながら、実際には犬の肉を売ってごまかすこと。**立派なものをおとりに使い、実際は粗悪なものを売ることの喩え。見かけと実質が伴わないことをいう。

近義詞 牛首を懸けて馬肉を売る ^{6級}　玉を衒いて石を売る ^{4級}

漢 掛羊頭賣狗肉。比喻以優質貨品做招牌，實際上兜售低劣的產品。以次充好，以假亂真，表裡不一，名不副實。

近 掛羊頭賣狗肉；金玉其外，敗絮其中

英 **Hanging up a sheep's head at the shopfront to sell dog's meat** (Chinese origin); Fig. What one sold is not what he said he was selling; To sell something that is inferior to what is claimed.

近 He cries wine and sells vinegar.; (a) pig in a poke; sail under false colors

---

287 寄らば大樹の陰 ^{6級}

日解與用法 雨宿りや日差しを避けるために樹の下に**身を寄せるのであれば、大木の下の方が良い。**頼る相手を選ぶならば、力のある者がよいということ。

近義詞 箸と主とは太いがよい ^{4級}　犬になるなら大家の犬になれ ^{4級}

漢 大棵樹樹枝葉茂盛，可以避雨或是乘涼。為了防曬避雨就要找顆大樹庇蔭。比喻若要投靠人要依附勢頭大的富貴人家，才有庇護。

近 大樹底下好乘涼；樹大好遮蔭；趨炎附勢

英 **To get in a big tree for shade** if you need to rest at a shelter from the rain or sun; Said if you need a patron, attach yourself to an influential person who can help.

近 It is good sheltering under an old hedge.; It never hurts to have friends in high places.

---

288 弱り目に祟り目 ^{6級}

日解與用法 **弱っている時に神仏の祟りに遭う。**転じて、困っている時にさらに災難に遭う、不運の上に不運が重なることの喩え。祟りとは、神々が下した処罰 (疫病、凶作、天災など) のこと。

近義詞 泣き面に蜂* ^{6級}　落ち目に祟り目 ^{4級}　転べば糞の上 ^{4級}

漢 脆弱無助的時候又遭天譴，雙重打擊。意指倒霉的事情不發生則已，一發生便接踵而至。

近 禍不單行；屋漏偏逢連夜雨，船遲又遇打頭風

英 **Divine retribution in one's hard time**; Indicates that bad things tend to happen in pairs, and not singly; If a person encounters bad luck, more bad luck will follow.

近 Misfortunes never come singly.; It never rains but it pours.

や行

289 来年のことを言えば鬼が笑う* [6級]

日解與用法 予知能力のある**鬼は、来年の話をする人間を見て**「明日のことすら分からないのに」と**笑い飛ばす**。「笑う」は馬鹿にする意。将来を予測できるわけがないのだから、先のことを言っても始まらないということの喩え。

近義詞 明日のことを言えば天井で鼠が笑う [4級]

[漢] 談論明年的事，連鬼都要偷笑。意指明天的事都無法預測，何況談明年的事。計劃言之過早將成為笑柄。

[近] —

[英] **If you talk of your resolution about next year, the orge will laugh at you.** A cliché to make fun of people who make a plan too early, as you don't even know what happen tomorrow, let alone predict for next year; It's useless to look things too far ahead.

[近] Fools set far trysts.

290 楽あれば苦あり [6級]

日解與用法 **楽しいことがあれば、苦しいこともある。**世の中は楽をしてばかりは過ごせない。苦楽相伴うのが人の世というものである。

近義詞 楽は苦の種、苦は楽の種 [4級]　人生、山あり谷あり [4級]

[漢] **有樂必有苦**，人生並非盡是樂事。苦樂是相伴而來的。

[近] （有苦必有樂）有樂必有苦；樂極生悲

[英] **After pleasure comes pain.** Where there is pleasure, there is pain. Life is not happy all the time, you cannot always be having fun.

[近] There is no pleasure without pain.; Life is not all beer and skittles.; There's no rose without a thorn.; You have to eat a peck of dirt before you die.

291 李下に冠を正さず [6級]

日解與用法 **スモモの木の下で手を上げて冠を直してはいけない。**他人からスモモを盗んでいるのではないかと疑われかねない。常に用心深くし、疑惑を招くような行為は慎むべきだということ。中国語の成語に由来。

近義詞 瓜田に履を納れず [6級]

[漢] 經過李樹下不要舉起手來撥正帽子，免得被誤為偷李子的小偷。比喻避免招惹無端的嫌疑。

[近] （瓜田不納履）李下不整冠

[英] **Don't fix your hat under a plum tree** (comes from a Chinese proverb); If you raise your hands, you might be accused of stealing plums. Used as an advice "Be careful not to invite the least suspicion".

[近] Caesar's wife must be above suspicion.; Abstain from all appearance of evil. (Bible)

ら行

292 竜頭蛇尾 _{6級}

日解與用法 頭は竜のように立派だが、尻尾は蛇のように細くて冴えない。初めは威勢が良かったが、終盤になるにつれて勢いがなくなる様子を喩える。

近義詞 頭でっかち尻つぼみ _{4級}

漢 龍頭蛇尾。指剛開始幹勁十足，聲勢赫奕，最後卻逐漸退縮而草率收尾。亦指做事有始無終。

近 龍頭蛇尾；虎頭蛇尾／虎頭鼠尾

英 **A dragon's head and a snake's tail.** Fig. A grand beginning and a tame ending. To start enthusiastically, but not properly complete the task. To end in an anticlimax. To end in smoke.

近 start with a bang and end with a whimper; go up like a rocket but come down like a stick

293 両手に花 _{6級}

日解與用法 美しい花を両手に持つ。同時に良いものを二つ占有することの喩え。また、一人の男性が二人の女性を連れている様子を言う。

近義詞 両手に旨い物 _{4級}

漢 雙手拿著花。比喻一個人獨佔兩個好東西，或引申為一位男士由兩位女士陪伴著。

近 享齊人之福

英 **Flowers in both hands**; To have two blessings at once; To gain advantage from both sides at the same time; Possibly interpreted when a gentleman is accompanied between two attractive ladies, like a cock of the walk.

近 butter both sides of one's bread

294 ローマは一日にして成らず _{6級}

日解與用法 ローマ帝国は一日のうちに建国されたものではない。築くに至るまでに、長い歴史があったことから、大事業は長年にわたる努力がなければ成し遂げられないという喩え。中世ラテン語のことわざに由来。

近義詞 千里の道も一歩より始まる* _{6級}

漢 羅馬非一朝一夕可建造成的，凡事都是經過長期累積逐漸醞釀而成的。喻成功不是一蹴可幾的。源自中世拉丁語的諺語。

近 羅馬不是一天造成的；冰凍三尺，非一日之寒

英 **Rome was not built in one day** (much-quoted medieval Latin adage); It took a very long time to build Empire of Rome, it wasn't built overnight. Said that any big projects or important things cannot be achieved instantly, but require time and patience.

近 Rome was not built in a day.

295 六十の手習い [6級]

日解與用法 六十歳になって字を習い始める意。老いてから勉学や芸事を始めること。

近義詞 八十の手習い* [5級]

漢 六十歲才開始學寫字。年紀大後才讀些書學點技藝。意指學無止境，一生虛心好學。

近 活到老，學到老

英 **To learn how to write at sixty**; Fig. There is no age limit for learning. You can always learn something new, because learning is a lifelong process, because knowledge is infinite.

近 You are never too old to learn.; It is never too late to learn.

---

296 論より証拠* [6級]

日解與用法 議論をするより証拠がものをいう。口先で議論を重ねるよりも、事実を明らかにする証拠を示した方が説得力があって話が早いということ。証拠は議論に勝る。

近義詞 論をせんより証拠を出せ [4級]

漢 事實證據勝於強辯。比喻事實證據比爭論更具有說服力。只要拿出證據，任何人都理屈詞窮，啞口無言。

近 事實勝於雄辯

英 **Evidence rather than debate.** Said to mean that you can only judge the truth of something after you have disclosed the proof of it. The facts speak for themselves and ultimately count.

近 The proof of the pudding is in the eating.; It speaks for itself.

---

297 若い時の苦労は買ってもせよ* [6級]

日解與用法 若い時にする苦労は自分を鍛え、成長に繋がるものだから、**金を出してでも求めるべきだ。**つまり、自ら進んで体験すべきとの教え。苦労を避けて楽に立ちまわるのは、将来の自分のためにならないという戒め。「若い時の苦労は買うてもせよ」ともいう。

近義詞 艱難汝を玉にす [3級]

漢 年輕時候的勞累辛苦，就算花錢買也是值得的。因為年輕時候的艱苦磨鍊可以造就自己，年紀大後就經不起磨鍊了。勸人趁年輕時多吃苦，先苦後甘。

近 少壯不努力，老大徒傷悲；寧吃少年苦，不受老來貧；黑髮不知勤學早，白頭方悔讀書遲

英 **Spare no effort while you are young.** Skills you learn as a young man don't wane as you grow older. If you live your youth years diligently, it will save you from regret when you are older. In addition, adversity put youself to the test, try to experience it as early as possible.

近 Diligent youth makes easy age.; Heavy work in youth is quiet rest in old age.; Reckless youth makes rueful age.; (A) young idler, an old beggar.

わ行

298 禍を転じて福と為す _{6級}

日解與用法 身にふりかかった**災難を**逆手にとって、それが**福に変わるように**取り計らう。災難に遭って悲嘆に暮れるより、それにうまく対処して幸いに逆転させることが重要である。中国の古典に由来。

近義詞 禍も幸いの端となる _{4級}

漢 把禍患變為幸福。提醒人災難臨頭或經歷挫折時要懂得如何對處以扭轉局勢，處之泰然才是重要。

近 轉禍為福；禍與福為鄰

英 **To turn one's misfortune into a blessing** (originated in a Chinese quote); To turn one's misfortune to account; To work to achieve positive results from a negative situation.

近 Make the best of a bad bargain.

299 渡りに船 _{6級}

日解與用法 どうやってこの**川を渡ろう**かと考えていたところ、**目の前に船が寄ってきた。**困っていたところに、都合よく望みどおりの条件が整うことをいう。『法華経』という仏教の経典にある言葉。

近義詞 干天の慈雨 _{4級} 闇夜の灯火 _{4級}

漢 正想過河，渡船剛好就來了。意指時機來得正好，正中下懷，凡事迎刃而解。源自佛教經典『法華經』。

近 及時甘霖；久旱逢甘露（他鄉遇故知）

英 Luck out with **a boat which takes you cross the river**; Said about rescue that cannot be more timely; like a godsend. Used when something fortunate occurs right when you need it most. (comes from the Buddhist Scripture "Lotus Sutra")

近 something that saves the day; (a timely) stroke of luck; like the rain after a long drought

300 笑う門には福来る* _{6級}

日解與用法 **笑いが満ちている家には幸福がめぐってくる。**いつもにこにこと笑って暮らす人の家は、明るくて和やかな雰囲気が漂う。

近義詞 笑って損した者なし _{4級} 和気財を生ず _{4級}

漢 和樂融融，笑聲不絕的家裡自然而然會招来福氣。意指和氣致祥，笑口常開笑臉迎人的人討人喜歡。

近 和氣生財；心寬體胖

英 **Fortune comes in at a smiling gate.** A cliché to express that time spent laughing is time spent in happiness.

近 Laugh and grow fat.; Cheerfulness is the very flower of health.; Be always as merry as you can, for few will delight in a sorrowful man. (17C); Laugh and the world laughs with you.

わ行

第三章

諺語紙牌遊戲
（いろはカルタ・以呂波歌留多・以呂波紙牌）

Iroha Karuta
(Japanese Playing Cards)

「いろはカルタ」古稱「いろは譬カルタ」，一套共計 96 張。原本是過年時孩童所玩的一種紙牌遊戲，目的是讓孩童透過遊戲來學習諺語。是以いろは 48 個字母（請參照下記解說）為開頭的一種紙牌，由印有諺語的 48 張「讀牌（字牌）」與印有諺語開頭第一個字和描繪該諺語內容的漫畫 48 張「抓牌（繪牌）」構成。玩法乃由一名參加遊戲的小孩將「讀牌」唸出來，由其他參加遊戲的小孩搶奪和「字牌」相符的「繪牌」，搶到較多紙牌的孩童為勝。這個紙牌的起源眾說紛紜，一般都認同是江戶末期之前（18 世紀後半）在上方（汎指現在的京都、大阪）開始製造的。

所謂「いろは字母」是日語平假名字母排列順序的一種方式。以大意如下的《以呂波歌》原文中不重複的平假名順序為排列依據。原文的 47 個平假名，最後加上「ん」字總共有 48 字。以前乃用來當日語字典的排列順序，在正式文書中也廣泛使用，但現在已經被五十音順（あいうえお順）取代。「いろは」則是此詩歌的前三個音。

いろはにほへと	ちりぬるを	色はにほへど	散りぬるを	花雖芬芳	總會凋落
わかよたれそ	つねならむ	我が世たれぞ	常ならむ	人生無常	孰可避免
うゐのおくやま	けふこえて	有為の奧山	今日越えて	塵世深山	今日翻越
あさきゆめみし	ゑひもせす	浅き夢見じ	酔ひもせず	妄夢不做	亦不沈醉

「カルタ」一詞來自葡萄牙語 carta（意指書簡、厚紙做成的撲克牌）。漢字可寫成「歌留多」或「紙牌」等等，相當於英語的 card。安土桃山時代（16 世紀中葉），透過貿易跟著槍枝、生絲、皮革、菸草一起從葡萄牙進口到九州的南蠻紙牌，經過日本人改良後所製作的就是「天正カルタ」，這是日本最初的國產紙牌。紙牌的生產後來轉移到京都這個大消費地區，由於經常被用於賭博，江戶時代曾多次遭到禁用。「歌留多」的詞源雖是葡萄牙語，但一般認為在日本和葡萄牙

交流之前，類似的紙牌遊戲即已存在。其歷史根源可以上溯至平安時代(12世紀左右)貴族之間玩的遊戲「貝覆い（貝殼配對遊戲）」。不久亦出現了「歌貝（和歌貝殼配對遊戲）」、「和歌カルタ（和歌紙牌）」等等遊戲。「カルタ（歌留多）」的出現給日本自古以來的配對遊戲帶來很大的改變。江戶時代風靡一時的就是賭博性質的遊戲紙牌「うんすんカルタ」，再而演變成教育性質的「いろはカルタ」。

　　兩張一對的「いろはカルタ（以呂波紙牌）」因製作年代和製作地點有別而蛻變了好幾次。京都製作的「京いろは（京都以呂波紙牌）」，在東京逐漸普及後，成為獨特的「江戶いろは（江戶以呂波紙牌）」。京都、尾張（名古屋）以及大阪的以呂波紙牌合流後則演變成俗稱「上方いろは（上方以呂波）」紙牌。根據文獻的記載，以「犬も步けば棒に当たる」開頭的江戶系統以呂波紙牌，在江戶時代末期大致固定為48句。上方系統以呂波紙牌則有相當多的變種，較為複雜。不只讀牌（字牌）如此、抓牌（繪牌）也有各種各樣的版本的漫畫。

京いろはかるた（複製品）
出典元：大石天狗堂

江戸いろはかるた（複製品）
出典元：大石天狗堂

到了明治大正時代，以呂波紙牌基於下述四項理由，紙牌的詞句不斷地被替換。

理由一：艱澀難懂。

理由二：帶有偏見和歧視的涵意。

理由三：粗俗不雅。

理由四：觀念不合時代。

紙牌原先的設計單純是為了讓孩童一面玩一面學會平假名、漢字、諺語和教訓，後來雖然因時代背景不同，有些詞句被替換掉。但為了一窺發行當時的江戶時代的文化，當時的代表性詞句仍為非常珍貴的考証資料。若讀者有興趣，可參考第 116-117 頁的一覽表，此為江戶時代流行的三種代表諺語語句。有一部分的詞句將於本書內介紹。

江戸初期 『婦女遊楽図屏風（松浦屏風)』国宝 大和文華館所蔵
出典元：江戸カルタ研究室

江戸初期 『かるた遊び図』 藤井永観文庫所蔵
出典元：江戸カルタ研究室

『風俗図』 たばこと塩の博物館所蔵
出典元：江戸カルタ研究室

江戶時代傳承至今的最具代表性之三種諺語紙牌詞句一覽

	江戶（東京） えど　とうきょう	上方（京都・大阪） かみがた　きょうと　おおさか	尾張（名古屋） おわり　なごや
い	犬も歩けば棒に当たる いぬ　ある　ぼう　あ	一寸先は闇（の夜） いっすんさき　やみ　よ	一を聞いて十を知る いち　き　じゅう　し
ろ	論より証拠 ろん　しょうこ	論語読みの論語知らず ろんご よ　ろんご し	六十の三つ子 ろくじゅう　み　ご
は	花より団子 はな　だんご	針の穴から天覗く はり　あな　てんのぞ	花より団子 はな　だんご
に	憎まれっ子世にはばかる にく　こ　よ	二階から目薬 にかい　めぐすり	憎まれっ子頭堅し にく　こ　かみかた
ほ	骨折り損のくたびれ儲け ほねお　ぞん　もう	仏の顔も三度 ほとけ　かお　さんど	惚れたが因果 ほ　いんが
へ	屁をひって尻すぼめ へ　しり	下手の長談義 へた　ながだんぎ	下手の長談義 へた　ながだんぎ
と	年寄りの冷や水 としよ　ひ　みず	豆腐に鎹 とうふ　かすがい	遠くの一家より近くの隣 とお　いっけ　ちか　となり
ち	塵も積もれば山となる ちり　つ　やま	地獄の沙汰も金次第 ぢごく　さた　かねしだい	地獄の沙汰も金次第 ぢごく　さた　かねしだい
り	律義者の子沢山 りちぎもの　こだくさん	綸言汗の如し りんげんあせ　ごと	綸言汗の如し りんげんあせ　ごと
ぬ	盗人の昼寝 ぬすびと　ひるね	糠に釘 ぬか　くぎ	盗人の昼寝 ぬすびと　ひるね
る	瑠璃も玻璃も照らせば光る る　り　はり　て　ひか	類をもって集まる るい　あつ	類をもって集まる るい　あつ
を	老いては子に従え お　こ　したが	鬼も十八 おに　じゅうはち	鬼の女房に鬼神 おに　にょうぼう　きじん
わ	破れ鍋に綴じ蓋 わ　なべ　と　ぶた	笑ふ門には福来る わら　かど　ふくきた	若いときは二度ない わか　にど
か	かったいの瘡うらみ かさ	蛙の面に水 かえる　つら　みず	陰うらの豆もはじけ時 かげ　まめ　どき
よ	葦のずいから天井のぞく よし　てんじょう	夜目遠目笠のうち よめとおめかさ	横槌で庭掃く よこづち　にわは
た	旅は道連れ世は情け たび　みちづ　よ　なさ	立て板に水 た　いた　みず	大食上戸餅食らい たいしょくじょうご もちく
れ	良薬は口に苦し りょうやく　くち　にが	連木で腹切る れんぎ　はらき	連木で腹切る れんぎ　はらき
そ	総領の甚六 そうりょう　じんろく	袖の振り合わせも他生の縁 そで　ふ　あ　たしょう　えん	袖の振り合わせも他生の縁 そで　ふ　あ　たしょう　えん
つ	月夜に釜を抜く つきよ　かま　ぬ	月夜に釜を抜く つきよ　かま　ぬ	爪に火をともす つめ　ひ
ね	念には念を入れよ ねん　ねん　い	猫に小判 ねこ　こばん	寝耳に水 ねみみ　みず
な	泣きっ面に蜂 な　つら　はち	なす時の閻魔顔 とき　えんまがお	習わぬ経は読めぬ なら　きょう　よ
ら	楽あれば苦あり らく　く	来年の事を言へば鬼が笑う らいねん　こと　い　おに　わら	楽して楽知らず らく　らく し
む	無理が通れば道理引っ込む むり　とお　どうりひ　こ	馬の耳に風 むま　みみ　かぜ	無芸大食 むげいたいしょく

う	嘘から出た真 うそ　　で　　まこと	氏より育ち うじ　　　そだ	牛を馬にする うし　　うま
ゐ	芋の煮えたもご存じない いも　に	鰯の頭も信心から いわし あたま しんじん	炒り豆に花が咲く い　まめ はな　さ
の	喉元過ぎれば熱さを忘れる のどもと す　　　　あつ　　　わす	鑿といわば槌 のみ　　　　つち	野良の節句働き の ら　 せっくばたら
お	鬼に金棒 おに　かなぼう	負うた子に教えられて浅瀬を渡る お　　こ　おし　　　　あさせ　わた	陰陽師身の上知らず おんようじみ　うえし
く	臭いものに蓋をする くさ　　　　ふた	臭いものに蝿がたかる くさ　　　　はえ	果報は寝て待て くゎほう　ね　ま
や	安物買いの銭失い やすものか　　ぜにうしな	闇に鉄砲 やみ　てっぽう	闇に鉄砲 やみ　てっぽう
ま	負けるが勝ち ま　　　か	蒔かぬ種は生えぬ ま　　　たね　は	待てば甘露の日和あり ま　　かんろ　ひより
け	芸は身を助く げい　み　たす	下駄と焼味噌 げた　やきみそ	下戸の建てた蔵はない げこ　た　　　くら
ふ	文はやりたし書く手は持たぬ ふみ　　　　か　て　も	武士は食わねど高楊枝 ぶし　く　　　たかようじ	武士は食わねど高楊枝 ぶし　く　　　たかようじ
こ	子は三界の首枷 こ　さんがい　くびかせ	これに懲りよ道才坊 こ　　　どうさいぼう	志は松の葉 こころざし　まつ　は
え	得手に帆を揚ぐ えて　ほ　あ	縁と月日 えん　つきひ	閻魔の色事 えん　いろごと
て	亭主の好きな赤烏帽子 ていしゅ　す　　あかえぼし	寺から里へ てら　　　さと	天道人殺さず てんどうひところ
あ	頭隠して尻隠さず あたまかく　　しりかく	足元から鳥が立つ あしもと　　とり　た	阿呆につける薬はない あほう　　　　くすり
さ	三遍回って煙草にしょ さんぺんまわ　　たばこ	猿も木から落ちる さる　き　　　お	触らぬ神に祟りなし さわ　　かみ　たた
き	聞いて極楽見て地獄 き　　ごくらくみ　じごく	義理と褌はかかねばならぬ ぎり　　ふんどし	義理と褌はかかねばならぬ ぎり　　ふんどし
ゆ	油断大敵 ゆだんたいてき	幽霊の浜風 ゆうれい はまかぜ	油断大敵 ゆだんたいてき
め	目の上の瘤 め　　うえ　こぶ	盲の垣のぞき めくら　かき	目の上の瘤 め　うえ　こぶ
み	身から出た錆 み　　　で　さび	身は身で通る み　　み　とお	蓑売りの古蓑 みのう　　ふるみの
し	知らぬが仏 し　　　ほとけ	しはん坊の柿の種 ぼう　かき　たね	尻食へ観音 しりくら　かんのん
ゑ	縁は異なものの味なもの えん　い　　　あじ	縁の下の舞 えん　した　まい	縁の下の力持ち えん　した　ちからも
ひ	貧乏暇なし びんぼうひま	瓢箪から駒 ひょうたん　こま	貧僧の重ね食い ひんそう　かさ　く
も	門前の小僧習わぬ経を読む もんぜん　こぞうなら　　きょう　よ	餅は餅屋 もち　もちや	桃栗三年柿八年 ももくりさんねんかきはちねん
せ	背に腹は代えられぬ せ　　はら　か	せんちで饅頭 まんじゅう	背戸の馬も相口 せと　うま　あいくち
す	粋は身を食う すい　み　く	雀百まで踊り忘れぬ すずめひゃく　おど　わす	墨に染まれば黒くなる すみ　そ　　　くろ
京	京の夢大坂の夢 きょう　ゆめおおさか　ゆめ	京に田舎あり きょう　いなか	

第四章

益智雙六遊戲
（すごろく・双六）

Sugoroku
(Japanese Board Game)

　　中國的古代遊戲黑白子的對戰棋盤遊戲「雙陸棋」，於奈良時代傳入日本後，名為「盤雙六」。而過年時孩童跟著大人一起玩的「繪雙六」，則又是另一種繪圖上的遊戲。一般即稱「すごろく（雙六或作双六）」。「繪雙六」的遊戲概念多多少少受「盤雙六」的影響，但自樹一幟。玩遊戲的人擲骰子在紙或布作的圖盤上，依骰子出現的數目挪步，每個格子都有「前進幾格」、「後退幾格」、「歇息一次」或「退回到起點」的指示，看誰最先走到終點誰就贏了。與中國傳統的昇官圖（只有文字沒有繪圖）或近代的大富翁類型的桌上遊戲比較相似。

　　據說，日本最早的繪圖漫畫型「繪雙六」是13世紀頃淨土宗的小沙彌想出來的。畫有極樂淨土故事的「淨土雙六」逐漸定型為「佛法雙六」，成為年輕僧侶學習的道具之一。到了江戶時代，出現了各式各樣題材的「繪雙六」。有旅遊指南（例如道中雙六，始於江戶日本橋，目的地為京都），有昇官遊戲（出世雙六，描述豐臣秀吉從一個賣針的少年發跡掌權至統一天下），有勸善懲惡的浮世繪武勇故事，有歌舞伎演員的肖像，連春宮畫也列入畫題。到了明治維新，為了教化國民，題材更多。例如天文地理、歷史人物、文學美術、風景名勝、環遊世界、諸國物產、英語、俄語單字等，可葷可素、無奇不有。

　　「繪雙六」的玩法有兩種，較簡單的迴紋針式雙六，與較複雜的跳格子式雙六。其實，「繪雙六」的遊戲概念確實也適合當教學教材，趣味無窮。雙六同時也是民眾的最愛。江戶至明治時代的「繪雙六」據說就超過120種，可以說是雙六歷史的黃金期。

江戸末期 『恋女房染分手綱』 歌川国貞作
ボストン美術館所蔵

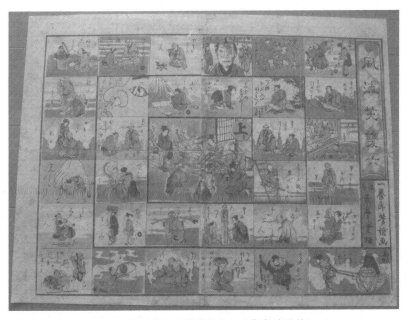

1865年 『風流笑雙六』 一養亭芳滝作
時田昌瑞ことわざコレクション 個人所蔵

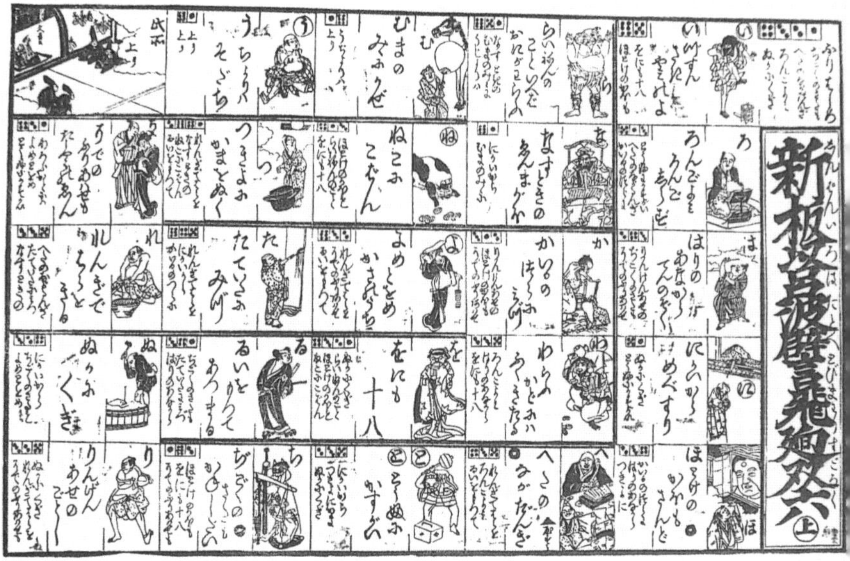

幕末〜大正時代 『新板以呂波譬飛廻雙六 上』 作者不明
時田昌瑞ことわざコレクション 明治大学博物館所蔵

幕末〜大正時代 『新板以呂波譬飛廻雙六 下』 作者不明
時田昌瑞ことわざコレクション 明治大学博物館所蔵

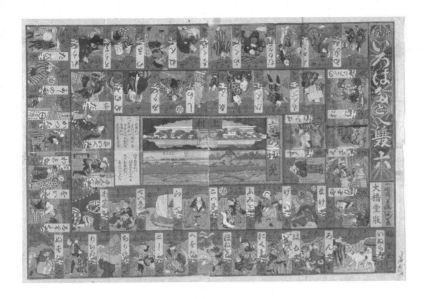

明治初期　『新版いろはたとへ雙六』　一鵬斉藤よし作
時田昌瑞ことわざコレクション　明治大学博物館所蔵

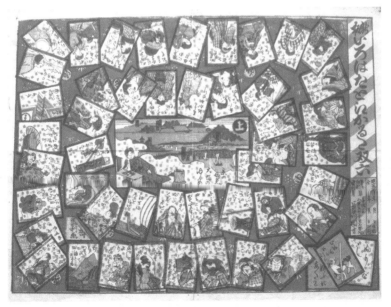

明治21年　『新版いろはたとへかるた双六』　長谷川園吉編
時田昌瑞ことわざコレクション　個人所蔵

江戸後期から発行された「ことわざ
尽くし」の典型的な一種。江戸系い
ろはカルタと殆どが重なる。

1862年 『教訓いろはたとへ』 歌川芳盛画
時田昌瑞ことわざコレクション 明治大学博物館所蔵

江戸後期から発行された「ことわざ尽
くし」の典型的な一種。江戸系いろは
カルタと殆どが重なる。芳盛には他に
も諺画の連作刷り物がある。幕末期に
最も多くの諺画を作成した絵師。

1862年 『教訓いろはたとへ』 歌川芳盛画
時田昌瑞ことわざコレクション 明治大学博物館所蔵

附錄

分級基準
日本「財團法人諺語能力檢定協會」擬定

Appendix
Criteria for the Classification of Levels

1級　大學～一般社會人士水平

既出版的成語諺語字典中未出現過的詞句，新發現的詞句，比較罕見、深澀難懂的詞句

例如：堅石も酔い人を避くる（古事記）、雉の頓使い（日本書紀）

2級　高中畢業～大學水平

源自世界各地的成語諺語詞句，源自日本的業界常用的成語諺語詞句

例如：好奇心は猫をも殺す（英語圏）、勘定合って銭足らず

3級　高中在學水平

古雅的成語諺語詞句、鄉土味重的成語諺語詞句、新創的成語諺語詞句

例如：衣食足れば則栄辱を知る、姑の留守は嫁の祭り（長野県）
赤信号皆で渡れば怖くない

4級　中學畢業水平

以高中升學考試常見的考題為中心，被視為教養須知，實用性高的成語諺語詞句

例如：薬も過ぎれば毒となる、重箱の隅を楊枝でほじくる

5級　中學在學水平

以中學升學考試常見的考題為中心，一般常用的基礎成語諺語詞句

例如：帯に短し襷に長し、初心忘るべからず

6級　小學畢業水平

以小學、中學升學考試常見的考題為中心，眾所周知的成語諺語詞句

例如：郷に入っては郷に従え、三人寄れば文殊の知恵

分級基準詳細請查閱參考「財團法人諺語能力檢定協會」的網頁
http://www.kotowaza-kentei.jp/index.html

注：協會於２０１１年「諺語檢定公式指南」發行後，將６級以上的詞句再
　　細分化成６～１０級。本書乃根據早期的１～６級分類。此外，著者於
　　編撰說明中曾提過，依專家觀點不同級數的分級標準頗有差距。因此，
　　本書中所標示的級數並非一種絕對值，僅是一種難易度的參考值。

日本語を母国語とする読者へ

　本書は、日本語を学んでいる中国語圏ならびに英語圏の方々のお役に立てるように構成されています。効果的に日本のことわざ・慣用句を学ぶために、中国語及び英語の直訳・意訳・類義語を添えています。皆様が、中国語圏や英語圏の方々と交流する際に、会話の種に本書を活用されることを願い、そして本書が自国日本のことわざ・慣用句の魅力を再発見するきっかけになってくれれば嬉しく思います。

　岩波書店の『広辞苑』では、ことわざを「古くから人々に言いならわされた言葉、教訓・諷刺などの意を寓した短句や秀句」と説明しています。『日本民族資料事典』では、「簡単な言葉で効果的に相手を納得あるいは屈服させようとする、一つのまとまった軽妙な文句である」と定義付けをしています。江戸時代にはことわざ・譬え・世話（俗語・熟語のような慣用的ことば）を分類せずに用いられて来たと考えられ、「慣用句」という概念（言葉）が明治時代以降にできたといわれています。本書ではことわざ以外に、慣用句も若干取り入れています。

　著者は本書で三つの言語における言葉の「ワザ」、「ひねり」を競演させられればと思っています。ことわざ・慣用句は、その国独特のものもあれば、各国に共通するものも数多くあります。　また、同じ表現が用いられても、文化の違いで全く異なった解釈をされる場合もあります。ここにこそ、ことわざ・慣用句を比較して深く知ることの面白さがあるのではないでしょうか。

　価値観や生活様式の変化により、ことわざ・慣用句の持つ意味が本来の意味から離れてしまったものも沢山あります。ことわざ・慣用句が生まれた当時は日常生活の中で（ことわざ・慣用句を）ごく普通に体験できましたが、現在では全く追体験できなくなったため、新しい解釈が生まれてくるのも理解できます。加えて、ことわざ・慣用句は「越境するもの」として知られています。本書で取り上げた300句のことわざ・慣用句は、日本に古くから伝わるものが主ですが、中国や西洋にその起源を持つものも少なくありません。従って、ことわざ・慣用句の本来の意味をしっかり理解した上で、時代に合った使い方が望ましいと著者は思います。先人達の英知やユーモアが凝縮されたこれらのことわざ・慣用句は、簡潔且つ説得力のあるレトリックであり、多くの人が国境を超えて考えや感情を共有することを可能にします。

　文化や歴史を反映していることわざ・慣用句を比較することで、世界中の人々がより深い相互理解を得られるようになると確信しています。また、この本が、皆様の語学学習の一助になることを心より願っています。

著者　日本東京にて

附録

To English native readers who understand Japanese or Chinese

The correct use of idioms and proverbs is one of the great things that distinguishes a native speaker from a non-native speaker.

Every language has pithy sayings which are integral and offer cultural essence. These sayings are called "idioms" and "proverbs". Learning idioms and proverbs can help you better understand the way people from a different culture think about the world. It's also intriguing to see how people express a truth or a belief based on their culture or the practical experience by using similes and metaphors.

An idiom or a proverb is a combination of words that you usually cannot understand just from the literal translation of individual words. For instance, if someone says, "Don't wake up a sleeping baby", they are not literally talking about a kid, what they mean is that "one should avoid talking about a bad situation that most people have forgotten about".

Certainly it requires some special cultural knowledge to understand idioms and proverbs, not just knowledge of vocabulary or grammar. Unless you really comprehend how to use idioms and proverbs in the correct context, you cannot become fully proficient in that language. You hear idioms and proverbs come all the time in different situations – on TV, in the news, in magazines and in newspapers, in formal speech or in informal daily conversation. If you are not able to catch the implication, you are definitely kept out of the loop.

This book includes 300 of the most commonly used idioms and proverbs to know. It also features adopted Chinese and English proverbs currently in use in Japanese. It is suited to learners of Japanese as their second language at all levels. By providing thorough explanations and stories about the origin of the idioms and proverbs, the learners can gain a much clearer insight into how the saying is used by native speakers. Besides, a comparison in English will help you grasp the sense of idioms and proverbs faster and better. In addition, you will be able to make a comparison with the equivalent Chinese proverbs provided too. I encourage you to do so, if you understand Chinese.

Please be aware that there may be some politically incorrect words in this book. I don't have any discriminatory intent but just want to convey how the proverbs have been used in the past. I hope you can enrich your Japanese conversation and get your point across to others by using some powerful expressions in this book.

From the author in Tokyo, Japan

附録

〈日文〉

荒屋勧監修　「子供も話す　実用中国語成語１０００」
　2001 年初版第 2 刷　光生館

稲田孝、他 6 名編　「中国の故事名言集」
　1997 年初版第 1 刷　平凡社

江川卓、他 60 名編　「世界の故事名言ことわざ総解説」
　2009 年改訂版第 9 版第 1 刷　自由国民社

大石学編著　「江戸時代のすべてがわかる本」
　2012 年第 4 刷発行　ナツメ社

大塚高信・高瀬省三編　「英語ことわざ辞典」
　1995 年初版第 1 刷　三省堂書店

奥津文夫著　「日英ことわざの比較研究」
　2000 年初版第 1 刷　大修館書店

小野忍、他 3 名編　「世界のことわざ辞典」
　1995 年第 39 版　永岡書店

金丸邦三編　「日中ことわざ対照集」
　1989 年再版　燎原書店

北原保雄編　「明鏡　ことわざ成句使い方辞典」
　2007 年初版第 1 刷　大修館書店

北村孝一訳　「絵解き　江戸庶民のことわざ」
　1991 年初版　東京堂出版

香坂順一著　「おぼえておきたい　中国語諺３００」
　1993 年初版第 1 刷　光生館

三省堂編修所編　「新明解　故事ことわざ辞典」
　2006 年第 7 刷　三省堂

清水勲編著　「江戸戯画事典」
　2012 年初版第 1 刷　臨川書店

附録

129

ジャン・マケーレブ、岩垣守彦編著 「英和イディオム完全対訳事典」
　　2003 年初版第 1 刷　朝日出版社

鈴木昶著 「かるた新・養生訓」
　　2006 年初版第 1 刷　青蛙房

尚学図書編集 「故事・俗信　ことわざ大事典」
　　1983 年第 1 版第 9 刷　小学館

庄司和晃著 「コトワザ教育のすすめ」
　　1987 年初版　明治図書

曾根田憲三著「映画で学ぶ英語ことわざ・慣用表現辞典」
　　1994 年初版第 1 刷　スクリーンプレイ出版

竹内靖雄著 「諺で解く日本人の行動学」
　　1999 年初版　東洋経済新報社

たつみ都志監修 「絵でわかる　ことわざ」
　　2009 年初版代刷　PHP 研究所

時田昌瑞著 「絵で楽しむ江戸のことわざ」
　　2005 年初版第 1 刷　東京書籍

時田昌瑞著 「図説　ことわざ事典」
　　2009 年第 1 刷　東京書籍

時田昌瑞著 「岩波ことわざ辞典」
　　2004 年第 10 刷　岩波書店

時田昌瑞著 「ことばで遊ぶいろはかるた」
　　2007 年初版第 1 刷　世界文化社

時田昌瑞監修 「親子で覚えることわざ教室」
　　2012 年初版第 1 刷　KK ベストセラーズ

中川志郎著 　「ことばの民俗学 – 動物」
　　1988 年第 1 刷　創拓社

附録

日本漢字教育振興会編　「漢検　四字熟語辞典」
　2008 年第 19 刷　日本漢字能力検定協会

浜慎二著　「頭が良くなるマンガ版ことわざ辞典」
　2008 年第 1 刷　三興出版

林四郎監修　「たのしく学ぶことわざ辞典」
　2004 年第 3 刷　NHK 出版

藤本義一・杉浦日向子著　「いろはカルタに潜む江戸のこころ・上方の知恵」
　1998 年初版第 1 刷　小学館

牧野高吉著　「英語イディオム表現集」
　2008 年第 1 刷　三修社

森隆夫・小宮山潔子　「ことわざ教育学」
　1984 年初版　チャイルド本社

森田誠吾著　「いろはかるた噺」
　1973 年第 1 刷　求龍堂

山口百々男編　「和英　日本ことわざ成語辞典」
　1999 年初版第 1 刷　研究社

山本忠尚監修　「新版　日英比較ことわざ事典」
　2012 年第 1 版第 4 刷　創元社

山本正勝著　「絵すごろく」
　2004 年初版第 1 刷　芸艸堂

米川明彦・大谷伊都子編　「日本語慣用句辞典」
　2006 年再版第 1 刷　東京堂出版

〈中文〉
姚義久編著　「慣用句諺語日語活用辭典」
　2013 年初版　大新書局 / 台灣

王永興編　「最新諺語俚語精華」
　2010 年初版　俊嘉文化出版事業 / 台灣

溫瑞政編 「中国谚语大全」
2004 年初版　上海辭書出版社 / 中國

溫惠雄編 「台灣人智慧俗語」
2005 年初版第 2 刷　宏欣文化出版事業 / 台灣

許晋彰，他 1 名編 「台灣俗語諺語辭典」
2009 年初版第 1 刷　五南圖書出版 / 台灣

鄭小飛，他 2 名編 「新編歇後語」
2005 年初版第 1 刷　漢宇國際文化出版 / 台灣

陳宗顯著 「台灣人生諺語」
2000 年初版第 1 刷　常民文化出版事業 / 台灣

張思本・高雅玲編 「日本諺語　順口溜」
2005 年初版第 1 刷　漢思有限公司 / 台灣

林昭文，他 3 名編 「台灣趣味諺語小百科」
2000 年初版　宇宙出版社 / 台灣

楊艷，他 2 名編 「中华谚语大词典」
2007 年初版第 2 刷　中國大百科全書出版社 / 中國

〈英文〉
AMERICAN SLANG DICTIONARY
　　Edited by Richard A. Spears
　　4th Edition　McGraw-Hill

BERMAN'S PROVERB WIT AND WISDOM
　　Edited by Louis Berman
　　1st Edition 1997　Perigee Trade

BREWER'S DICTIONARY OF PHRASE & FABLE
　　Revised by John Ayto
　　17th Edition 2005　Weidenfeld & Nicolson, The Orion Publishing Group

附
錄

CAMBRIDGE – INTERNATIONAL DICTIONARY OF IDIOMS
    Edited by Cambridge University
    1st Edition 1998   Cambridge University Press

NTC'S DICTIONARY OF PROVERBS & CLICHÉS
    Compiled by Anne Bertram / Edited by Richard A. Spears
    1996 National Textbook Company

NTC'S AMERICAN IDIOMS DICTIONARY
    Edited by Richard A. Spears
    3rd Edition 2000 NTC Publishing Group

OXFORD DICTIONARY OF ENGLISH IDIOMS
    Edited by John Ayto
    3rd Edition 2010 Oxford University Press

THE OXFORD DICTIONARY OF ENGLISH PROVERBS
    Revised by William. G. Smith
    3rd Edition 1980   Oxford University Press

THE PROVERBS AND EPIGRAMS OF JOHN HEYWOOD, A.d. 1562
    Edited by John Heywood
    2007 Kessinger Pub. Co.

THE ROUTLEDGE BOOK OF WORLD PROVERBS
    Compiled by Jon R. Stone
    1st Edition 2006 California State University Press

WICKED WORDS
    Edited by Hugh Rawson
    1989   Crown Publishing Group

其の他各種日本語辞書、中日辞書、和英辞書、英和辞書、英英辞書も参考にした。
講談社：日本語大辞典、三省堂：広辞林、ＴＢＳブリタニカ：ブリタニカ国際大
百科事典、角川書店：新国語辞典、小学館：新選漢和辞典、大修館：漢語新辞典、
三省堂：デイリーコンサイス英和辞典、川出書房：日本 / 中国 / 西洋 / 故事物語、
新星出版社：故事ことわざ辞典、学習研究社：故事ことわざ辞典、Canon：国語
/ 和英 / 英和 / 漢和 / 電子辞典等々。

日文索引 Japanese Phrase Finder Index

う

索引

索引

137

索引

索引

141

索引

索引

143

索引

144

中文索引　Chinese Phrase Finder Index

5劃

8 劃

9劃

12劃

索引

157

B

索引

索引

E

索引

163

H

索引

索引

Q

R

S

索引

T

索引

171

索引

173

Y

索引

後記

　　此書由撰寫原稿至上梓出版約花了兩年半的歲月。2014年初秋拿著半完成的稿子造訪台北大新書局林駿煌董事長，毛遂自薦地介紹自己研究諺語的經緯。未料林董事長當場對此書甚感興趣，除鼓勵我出版以外並提供許多寶貴的意見，使我受寵若驚。沒有林董事長的提拔，此書恐怕終世不見天日。

　　執筆本書時亦蒙文學素養非常高的穗高先生和編集經驗資深的渡邊女士協助日文校對，還有立教大學英文講師的George老師協助英文校對，謹此向各位深深致謝。同時亦感謝收藏家時田先生，明治大學博物館學藝員外山先生，提供江戶時代的諺語相關圖像，給此書更添精彩。

著者簡歷

上野潤子 1953 年生。
東京外國語大學日本語學科畢業。
造紙工業技術文獻專業翻譯家。
策劃華語‧英語企業研修教材。
日本ことわざ文化學會‧ことわざ學會會員。
「ことわざ再発見倶楽部」主宰。

錄音

清水裕美子

成語諺語精選 300 則

2016 年(民 105) 12 月 1 日 第 1 版 第 1 刷 發行

定價 新台幣:380 元整

著　　者　上野潤子
發 行 人　林 駿 煌
封面設計　趙 乙 璇
發 行 所　大新書局
地　　址　台北市大安區 (106) 瑞安街 256 巷 16 號
電　　話　(02)2707-3232‧2707-3838‧2755-2468
傳　　真　(02)2701-1633‧郵政劃撥:00173901
法律顧問　中新法律事務所　田俊賢律師

香港地區　香港聯合書刊物流有限公司
地　　址　香港新界大埔汀麗路 36 號 中華商務印刷大廈 3 字樓
電　　話　(852)2150-2100
傳　　真　(852)2810-4201